Freedom's Distant Frontier

LACY WILLIAMS

Chapter One

ONE BREATH.

Then another.

Each rasped through Lily Fairfax's throat, shallow and uneven.

The wagon swayed beneath her, its wooden frame groaning as it trundled over the difficult mountain pass. The motion tugged at memories of an ocean crossing—weeks aboard a creaking ship, Lily's stomach roiling with seasickness and her heart aching for Ireland. For the familiar.

She pressed her cheek deeper into her folded arms, her thoughts a maelstrom.

Why had she left home? Stella had promised a new life, a better one, for her and Maddie in America. A fresh start. But her older sister's promises had crumbled to dust.

Harry was gone. Dead.

Lily's chest tightened. How could she still breathe? How could her heart still beat when it was broken?

The wagon jolted hard, boards creaking beneath her. She lay prone, belly pressed to the bedroll, and barely shifted with the lurch. Surrounded as she was by boxes and crates and barrels, there was nowhere to go.

Outside, Stella's voice cut through the dusk, sharp with command as she halted the oxen. The wheels slowed, grinding to a stop on the rocky earth.

Lily stayed still, listening to the thud of her own pulse, the murmur of her sisters' voices beyond the canvas, the distant calls of pioneers circling up for the night. She tipped her head, a sliver of fading light pierced the gap in the wagon's cover. Days had grown shorter in these mountains, but the journey stretched endlessly ahead, even after months of travel. Would it ever end?

A fierce wave of nausea surged. Lily swallowed against it, her hand sliding beneath her abdomen. Her eyes fluttered shut, willing the storm inside her to quiet. She couldn't do this.

Maddie's voice drifted closer, still outside the wagon, soft but clear. "Jason took the boys to check on a patient. Is Lily still resting in the wagon?"

Stella's reply was sharp as a whip crack. "She's been abed like a lazybones. We need to do something, Maddie."

Did Stella mean for Lily to hear? The thought pricked, stirring her from the haze.

Maddie murmured something too low to catch.

Stella's voice remained pitched to carry. "The journey doesn't pause for grief. She needs to get up. Carry her weight. It isn't fair to you or me—"

The words ignited something inside Lily, pushing her to sit upright. She raised her hand to her head and fought off the momentary dizziness. Her limbs trembled as she wrapped her knitted shawl around her shoulders. She shoved the wagon flap aside and stepped into the clamor of camp. Wagons sat in a circle, children darted past with high-pitched laughs, and a dog barked somewhere near the fire. The air smelled of smoke and pine.

Stella and Maddie glanced up from where they crouched by a smoldering fire, kindling catching with faint pops.

Maddie's eyes widened, a guilty flush creeping up her cheeks. "Lily! Are you feeling all right?"

"I'm not sure it matters, at least not to Stella. Your worker bee is here." Lily's words held a snap, and her lip curled, grief simmering too close to the surface. "Perhaps now you can stop talking about me."

Stella straightened, brushing soot from her hands. She looked pale and exhausted, and for a moment, Lily was reminded of the baby her sister carried. "If you'd come out of the wagon once in the past three days, we wouldn't be so concerned."

"Concerned? Is it concern that dismisses my grief?" Lily's voice rose with the ache in her chest.

Stella's mouth tightened. She waved a hand toward the bustling camp. "We came here for a fresh start. So did they. You're not the only one who's lost something."

The words cut deep, slicing through the tender places inside Lily.

Maddie reached out, fingers hovering near Stella's arm, but the damage was done.

"What have you lost?" Lily burst out, her voice quaking. "You've gained a husband. You have a child on the way. Maddie's got her new family. I'm the only one who's suffered a great loss."

Stella shook her head, her frown deepening. "I can understand losing a friend—"

"Harry was more than a friend!" Lily's outburst drew the gaze of an older man unloading a crate nearby. Ezra Simmons.

Stella's skepticism shadowed her face. "You barely knew him."

Maddie tugged at Stella's sleeve, but Lily's words spilled free. "We were going to marry. And—I'm carrying his child."

The confession hung in the air between them, filling the sudden silence.

Harry hadn't promised marriage, not in so many words. She'd thought there'd be time.

Maddie's expression stayed steady, unsurprised. Had she known?

Stella's cheeks flushed crimson. "What?"

Her sharp question turned more heads in the camp. Stella noticed, lowering her voice as she demanded, "How could you? Didn't Maddie and I teach you better?"

New hurt swelled, threatening to choke Lily. "It was never your job to raise me. Maybe we'd all be better off if you hadn't tried."

The words fell like stones into still water, rippling through the silence.

Stella's face paled.

Maddie looked as if she would say something, but now that the dam was broken, Lily's words tumbled over each other. "I never wanted to come to America. You insisted. You told me and Maddie it was our best chance for a new future. But you've put us in danger over and over. In New York, those awful men were after us. Then a tornado nearly struck our wagon. You've ruined our lives."

The wilderness was vast and frightening. There would be no town or city when they finally reached the Willamette Valley. She'd never once had the chance to wear the fancy dress she'd bought in New York before they'd had to run.

Stella stared, her face a mask. Then she folded her hands at her waist, voice steady as iron. "Every choice I've made was to protect you. To provide for you. One day you'll appreciate what I've done." She turned and strode away, boots crunching on the gravel.

Lily's knees buckled. Tears slipped free, dripping onto her dress as she sank to the ground. The flood she'd held back broke loose, overwhelming her. She couldn't wipe the tears fast enough, her hands trembling against her cheeks.

Maddie came closer, skirts rustling as she settled beside Lily. Her hand rested warm on Lily's shoulder through the shawl.

"Harry loved me," Lily whispered, voice breaking. "I kept our relationship a secret..." The story tumbled out—

Harry's charm, his tender promises, the moments that had bound them.

When her words ran dry, her tears had slowed. She hid her face in her arms.

Maddie squeezed Lily's shoulder gently. "I'll help you," she murmured.

Lily's heart twisted. Maddie couldn't promise that—not with her duties working beside Jason, the wagon train's doctor. Maddie worked as camp nurse, tending to the wagon train company day and night. Lily was surprised they had been undisturbed for this long. Shouldn't the doc be calling for Maddie already?

Lily lifted her chin from her knees, face tight and hot from crying. "Shall I interrupt you mid-birthing to say I'm frightened of a stampede? Or that a storm's coming?"

Maddie's lip parted, but Lily pressed on, bitterness sharp in her belly. "Since Stella married Collin, I've been alone. Harry saw me. He cared when I was frightened and lonely. He was there. And now I have no one."

A tiny cry pierced the air from Maddie's wagon nearby.

Maddie sighed, muttering, "We aren't done," and rose, brushing dirt from her skirt. She returned moments later, Jenny bundled in her arms. Maddie and Jason had only been married two weeks ago, but they had adopted the one-year-old along with her two older brothers, Paul and Alex.

Lily stared into the flickering flames. She hadn't meant to say the thought aloud—*I have no one*—but saying the words made truth crash over her. It stole her breath and she couldn't catch it back.

Her chest locked tight, dark spots dancing at the edges of her vision. Dizziness swept in.

Before Lily could ask, Maddie spread a blanket behind Lily, away from the fire's heat. She guided Lily to lie back, settling beside her, shoulder pressing warm against Lily's.

"Count this breath with me," Maddie said firmly. "One, two, three..."

The rhythm tugged Lily back to Dublin, to a night when she'd been fourteen, lying beside Maddie in the lumpy bed in their cramped tenement room. They'd waited for Stella, disguised as a man, after her first day of working in the factory. That day, Lily's panic had gripped her the same way it did now, choking off her breath.

Maddie's steady voice had calmed her then.

As her breathing eased, the stars above sharpened into focus. Maddie's hand clasped hers in the space between them, a firm anchor.

Where was Jenny? Lily tilted her head and saw the little one nestled against Maddie's chest, thumb in mouth, quiet now.

"You aren't alone," Maddie whispered. "You've got me. I'll always be your sister."

The words should've warmed her, but Lily knew Maddie's heart was spoken for by Jason and her adopted children. She deserved that joy.

Lily's hand rested on her belly, still flat but hiding a secret too big to fathom. A baby. Alone. Without Harry.

What was she going to do?

* * *

How hard could it be to find one little ruby?

The sun hung low over the jagged peaks, painting the sky with streaks of gold and casting long shadows. Matt Grayson shifted in the saddle of the dun gelding he rode on the outskirts of the mass of plodding cattle. Afternoon was waning. The herd of cattle moved restlessly in the narrow valley, clumping in one big bunch, as the train of wagons navigated the terrain.

Matt still wasn't used to this life. He'd been hired on four weeks ago, a job necessary to his real task—finding that ruby for Amos Byrnes. His boss had sent three men after the ruby once he'd realized it was missing from his safe. After weeks had gone by without any sign of his men's return, Amos had tasked Matt with bringing it back.

He'd taken what little information he'd had and followed the women's trail to Independence. He was weeks behind them at the jumping off point for the wagons, but riding solo across the prairie, often riding day and into the night had allowed him to catch up with the company at one of the forts, where he'd hired on with Leo and Collin.

If Matt had expected this job to be easy, he'd been sorely mistaken. Since he'd joined the hired hands, no one in the entire company had breathed a mention of the ruby. And he didn't dare ask—he wasn't supposed to know the jewel existed. If he was found out, he'd likely be hanged or abandoned by the company. He'd realized early on that the isolation out here in the wilderness meant danger; everything wanted to kill a man.

Matt had worked for Amos Byrne for a dozen years now. He'd always done what was needed. But of all the jobs he'd done for his boss, none had ever taken this long. And unlike his jobs in New York, the population of this company was small—about two hundred travelers. Everyone knew everyone else by name. There was nowhere to hide, even for someone used to staying in the shadows, like Matt.

Before leaving New York, he hadn't known how to ride. He'd spent a day in Independence learning this horse and the basics of riding horseback. He still didn't sit a saddle as easy as the other cowboys.

Ahead, a steer broke from the herd, lumbering through the scrub, hooves snapping dry twigs with a crack that echoed in the still air. Matt reined his horse to follow, sharp edge of frustration growing inside him. He wasn't cut out for this wild sprawl. He was sunburned, smelled like a horse, hadn't slept in a real bed in months.

"Get on, you ornery cuss," he muttered, leaning low in the saddle.

But the steer sidestepped, jogging off in the opposite direction, tail flicking like a taunt.

Irritation coiled tighter in Matt's chest.

He needed to find that ruby and get back to New York City.

The steer bolted again, and Matt yanked on the reins, his horse snorting a plume of breath into the cooling air. His patience was fraying when a voice rose beside him.

"You know, son, there's a Bible tale about a fellow who strayed far from home." Rusty grinned from the back of his gray and white dappled horse that matched the steer's every move.

Not this again.

Matt shifted in the saddle, blocking the steer with Rusty's help. The animal finally gave in and moved back toward the rest of the herd.

"Prodigal son, you heard of him?" Rusty asked as he settled his horse next to Matt's. "Left his pa, squandered everything on wild living. Ended up feeding pigs, starving and broke. But when he came back, his pa ran out to meet him—threw a feast."

"I'm not in the mood for one of your stories," Matt said. But there was no conviction in his voice.

Since Harry had died a few days ago, the mood in the cowboy camp had shifted to something more serious. Gone were the nights full of laughter and camaraderie. Now there was a contemplative silence and long brooding stares from the other four men hired to watch over the cattle for Leo Spencer on this journey.

"You sure?" Rusty asked.

Matt shrugged. "Ain't got no folks. Stories like that don't mean much to me."

Rusty's expression was hard to read, and Matt didn't need pity. He'd done all right for himself, even though he'd been on his own since he was a young pup. He nudged his horse forward, and Rusty followed the steer back to the herd proper. Three more cows started off, and Rusty gave chase.

Matt followed the herd, eyeing the wagons slowly making their way up the rocky incline. Coop Spencer rode up, relaxed in the saddle. "Creek up ahead. Going to rest the cattle for a bit. Let them have a drink. Reckon your canteen needs filling, too."

Matt would welcome the chance to get off the horse. Even after weeks on the trail, his back and legs still ached after every long day in the saddle.

Coop was the twin brother of Collin Spencer—the man married to the thief who'd taken the ruby from Amos's safe back in New York City. Collin was laid back, except when it came to his wife.

Matt had followed a badly drawn sketch of Stella Fairfax across the plains and all the way to the fort. He'd pieced things together after joining up with Hollis's company. Apparently, Stella and her sister Lily had disguised themselves as men when they had joined up with the company in Independence, Missouri. From what he could gather, it hadn't been long before they'd been found out. Collin had married Stella.

As Coop rode with one eye on the herd, Matt said in as casual a voice as he could muster, "Company seems exhausted and scared. We need another sing-along like we had before."

Coop was distracted, his eyes narrowed as he watched the wagons. What was he looking for? "That's not going to happen until we get over this pass," he glanced at Matt, "and that'll be weeks yet at the pace we're going."

A thump of defeat. Matt didn't have weeks. It was a rare

evening when the company stopped and everyone gathered for music and visiting. That would be a perfect opportunity to search the Fairfax wagon, where Matt guessed the ruby was hidden. But if that wasn't going to happen anytime soon, perhaps he needed to figure a different way to get close to that wagon.

Coop spotted his brother Collin, nudged his mare into a trot, and left Matt staring at the wagons. He caught sight of the Fairfax wagon. He knew it because one of the hoops that held up the canvas at the back of the wagon had been bent before he had joined up.

Lily Fairfax walked beside the oxen, her shawl wrapped around her, head low.

He'd been coming off watch a week ago when he nearly stumbled over her snuggled with Harry. In a split second, a snake bite had taken the other man's life. He still couldn't forget her tearful demand that Matt help, even as Harry's life expired.

Matt had woken every night since with her grief-stricken cry echoing in his mind, straining his ears for the sound of anything slithering in the grass.

Maybe it was the twilight, but she looked like a shadow of the vibrant young woman he'd watched for weeks, looking for a moment he might take advantage of to find that ruby. She looked like a strong wind might blow her over. Harry's sudden and violent death reminded him that he needed to find that ruby and make tracks.

Stella was rarely without her husband, and she was fierce in her own right. Confronting her meant he was likely to get himself shot. Maddie, the third sister, married to the Doc and mother to three children orphaned by typhoid, was busy all hours nursing folks. She also had a protective husband.

The rhythmic sound of horse's hooves pulled Matt's attention away from the wagons. It was Rusty again, riding up beside him. No doubt ready to share another Bible story that Matt didn't care to hear.

One more glance at Lily twisted his gut in a way he couldn't explain. She was often on her own. He wouldn't try to woo her, not with the loss of her beau. But maybe he could befriend her. Get close enough to find out where the Fairfax sisters had stashed that ruby.

* * *

Coop Spencer hadn't touched a bottle in over a week. Hadn't touched a flask. Or a jar.

And he was completely fine. He'd sweated through both his shirt and his bedroll those first two nights of fitful sleep. But now he wasn't thinking about having a drink every second of the day.

Mostly because he was fixated on finding his mystery girl. Woman, actually.

Even now, when he was keeping his hands busy building a fire for the hired hands and readying the coffeepot, he couldn't seem to stop his eyes from scanning the nearby wagons.

Two little kids played tag near one wagon, a couple chickens pecking the ground nearby. Not far away, an older woman scolded her husband while he worked with a chisel on a piece of wood. The old guy seemed to be ignoring her.

No shadows moved in the waning afternoon sunlight. Was Coop's mystery girl hiding in a wagon? Maybe buried beneath crates and blankets?

His imagination had conjured up a hundred places she could be since he'd grabbed her outside the circle of wagons. He'd thought for sure she was a thief, but her instant fear had prompted him to let go of her when she'd pulled away.

Something he now regretted.

He'd questioned several of the folks when he'd had a chance. Few of them seemed curious, all exhausted and weary of the constant travel. None had any patience for his self-imposed quest.

Ain't no young woman in this campsite. You musta been seeing things.

That had been Rusty's assumption when Coop had asked the other cowhand to keep his eyes open around camp.

No one believed Coop had seen the mystery girl. But he knew he wasn't crazy.

He hadn't imagined nearly drowning in a little creek when he'd been drunk as a skunk. Or the woman who'd saved him. He hadn't imagined coming face to face with her, even if it was dark.

But now she'd disappeared.

That night he'd almost died had been a wake up call. He couldn't let himself get so drunk that he lost control of his bodily functions. That he couldn't remember what'd happened in his drunken stupor. Maybe one or two drinks would do—take the edge off. Help him forget about the cuts on his insides that never seemed to stop stinging with hurt no matter what he tried.

Coop caught motion out of the corner of his eye and quickly turned his head, hope surging warm in his chest—only to fade. Not her.

Coop's twin brother, Collin, stomped toward the circle of wagons from where he'd helped the cowboys settle the herd of seventy cattle for the night. Coop knew that jut of his twin's jaw, the temper simmering beneath a tight lid, ready to spill. Lately, Collin's ire turned on him too often. Collin was just like their older brother Leo, who walked around in a constant state of disappointment at Coop's choices.

His sister Alice was the only one who seemed compassionate to his plight. Bless her.

Coop rose swiftly, brushing soot from his palms. He slipped into the woods, the cool shade swallowing him as he left the fire's glow behind. A wash at the creek was reason enough—trail dust clung thick, especially riding drag, the worst task. Every particle of grit seemed to gather at his collar, stick to the sweat on his neck, and itch beneath his shirt.

The creek murmured ahead, a silver thread winding through the trees. Coop stepped into the clearing, the trickle of water glinting in the dusk. Young Ben waded there, skirt knotted high above her knees, her legs splotched red from the cold's bite. August Mason crouched on the bank, head tilted slightly, his broad frame steady despite the blindness that had claimed him two weeks past when a gunpowder barrel exploded in a flash of fire and smoke. Ben didn't see Coop, her back to him as she splashed, but August's chin lifted, eyes staring past him—unfocused, searching.

"It's me," Coop murmured, stepping closer, boots soft on the mossy earth.

Tension eased from August's shoulders, a faint line melting from his frame. "Everything all right? Felicity holding up?" His voice was husky and low.

Coop's gut twisted as he remembered just how fierce August had been when Felicity faced peril. August had demanded Coop's help, uncompromising and almost wild in his need to rescue his woman. In the days after their prairie wedding, he'd stuck close to her. Protective.

Now that the blast had stolen his sight, August was like a shadow of himself.

"Dunno," Coop admitted, rubbing his neck. "Didn't see her 'fore I left camp."

August's chin tipped up, a faint crease between his brows. "Running from Collin again?"

"Not running." Coop rolled his shoulders. "Just need a wash."

August shook his head slightly, turning toward Ben, who'd splashed downstream a dozen yards, her giggles threading through the trees. Suddenly, she bent, grasping at the water near her feet, and toppled to her knees with a splash, droplets flying like scattered stars. August didn't flinch, his face still, and Coop held his breath as she stood, shaking wet hands, water dripping from her elbows. She laughed, unbothered, and squatted again, peering into the stream's flow.

"Want me to check on her?" Coop asked after a moment that stretched long.

"She need it?"

"Guess not."

Ben's hum floated back, steady as she poked the water.

Coop couldn't help asking, "What if she wanders too far?"

The woods were a tangle of branches and shadows. These mountains were less forgiving than the prairie the company had crossed weeks past.

August's hand fisted at his side, though his voice stayed mild. "She's louder than a penned hog. I'd hear her."

"Is she?" Coop strained, catching only her splashes and the creek's soft gurgle.

August nodded, fingers trailing the water's edge, swirling the current. "If there were a passel of young'uns around, I'd lose her in the clamor. But I've a sense of her—her steps, the splash when she moves, that hum she makes when she's thinking."

The way he described hearing his adopted daughter gave Coop a sudden idea. "You been hearing anything odd around camp?"

August cocked his head, brow furrowing slightly.

"Leo mentioned missing food. You catch anything strange? At night, maybe?" Coop pressed on, words tumbling free as the thought took root. He had to be careful how he brought this up—August's brother, Owen, was Leo and Alice's half brother and was one of the captains for the company.

August's frown deepened. "Thought that'd stopped."

Had Coop scared her into hiding? Was she starving to remain unseen?

"Say I wanna find this... person," he said, leaning closer, voice low over the creek's murmur. "I've watched every corner of camp these past days, looking for a sign—any trace. But I haven't found anything. You're a tracker—"

"Not anymore." A snap of resignation shadowed August's tone, stirring an ache in Coop's own heart, an echo of loss he knew too well.

"Surely you ain't forgotten everything you know." He didn't know whether he meant to figure out a way to find the mystery woman or to put out the fire that must be burning inside the other man.

"When I'm tracking in the woods," August began, "I don't see the prey. I see the evidence. A bent piece of grass where they brushed against it. A track in soft soil. It isn't *them*, it's the sign they left behind."

Sign.

What sign would the mystery girl have left behind?

"Like a blanket where she's been sleeping," Coop murmured.

"She?" August echoed.

"Or footprints by the creek."

She'd been alone in the woods late at night. He knew it,

because she'd saved him. But he hadn't really thought about what it meant until just now.

Was she following the company rather than hiding somewhere among the wagons? Maybe he was looking in all the wrong places.

Fresh excitement made him slap his thighs and straighten, ready to go search.

"Sometimes there's a reason a body don't want to be found." The sudden, unexpected words from August stopped Coop in his tracks. But only for a moment.

"I'll see ya later," he said. "Have fun, Ben!" he called out.

Maybe August was right and the mystery girl didn't want to be found. But Coop couldn't forget the instant recognition he'd felt throughout his whole body the moment he'd come face-to-face with her.

He owed her. A life debt, really.

He could help her.

He just had to find her.

Chapter Two

MATT JUMPED at an unexpected clatter from one of the wagons parked nearby.

The sun had dipped low, brushing the camp with a golden glow as the wagons were still circling up. Lucky had scouted a quiet patch—the only grassy spot for miles—where the cattle could graze overnight, and the other cowboys were herding the cattle that way, their shouts rising sharp over the lowing of the beasts. Coop and Matt had been tasked with setting up the camp and getting supper going.

The cowboys would come to the campfire hungry.

As Matt squatted again near the fire he was trying to light, Coop stalked the edge of camp, sweeping his foot through sparse grass. He must be looking for firewood. He was usually jovial but hadn't joined them at the fire to share a flask in several nights. Maybe he was as shaken up about Harry's death as all the other men.

"You all right?" Matt asked.

Before Coop could answer, Collin rode up and dismounted. Matt watched as Coop's shoulders wound even tighter.

"Can you go unhitch Stella's oxen?" Weariness edged Collin's voice, his attention still on the cattle being pushed to their home for the night.

Coop bent to scoop up another piece of wood, a flicker of defiance in his stance. "Lily was driving oxen earlier."

"She's still at it." Collin's jaw tightened, and he glanced at Matt. Everyone in camp could see the tension between the two brothers. Was he ashamed of it?

Collin went on, "The beasts are too big for her to turn out proper."

"Why can't you do it? She's your sister-in-law," Coop shot back.

"I'm asking you to do it."

Coop opened his mouth to refuse, and Matt found himself standing, blurting out, "I can do it." He fought to keep his voice casual. "The fire is lit. There's potatoes and meat in the cook pot."

Coop kept on with his task while Collin speared Matt with a stare. Collin gave his brother one more hard look, and then his expression shifted into one of resignation. "Fine." He mounted up and rode off.

Matt dusted his hands on his thighs, and Coop didn't give him another glance as he strode off toward the pioneer camp. The cowboys always kept a little distance, preferring to keep things a little more rowdy and real at their campfire.

Plus, they took turns watching the cattle overnight. It wouldn't be a full night in a bed, no matter where that bed was.

The camp buzzed with life—men hollered orders as the last of the wagons joined the circle, children underfoot. Matt wove through the melee, anticipation building as he approached the Fairfax wagon. The wagon was at a stop, the oxen patient in their traces, the wood groaning faintly as the beasts shifted their weight. Lily was nowhere in sight. His pulse kicked up, but he kept a calm façade. He glanced around, but no one spared him any attention, all focused on fires and bedrolls.

"Hello?" he called.

The nearest ox twitched an ear, but nothing else stirred. Maybe she'd gone to the creek to wash up or fetch water. Matt circled the wagon, his steps deliberate, aware of the older couple talking in low voices at their fire nearby.

No sign of Lily. No eyes on him.

A chance like no other.

Ears alert for the crunch of approaching footsteps, he stepped to the front of the wagon and boosted himself onto the wheel spokes. He tugged the canvas loose only to find the shadowed inside a jumble of crates and barrels. Something hung from the ceiling poles; clothing swung faintly in the breeze. In the back corner, a fancy concoction of pale blue fabric and lace waved minutely in an invisible breeze.

Amos had told him that the ruby was roughly the size of a robin's egg and mounted on a gold chain. It was worth a fortune, so the Fairfax sisters wouldn't leave it in plain sight.

It could be tucked anywhere in this clutter, hidden in a seam or crate's corner.

Matt's fingers brushed the wagon's corner, hoping lady luck would smile on him.

"What are you doing?" The sharp female voice jolted him. He hopped down, forcing an easy smile. Lily stood near the back of the wagon, eyes narrowed and arms crossed tight over her middle, her shawl obscuring most of her dress.

"Collin asked me to unhitch the oxen," Matt said.

Her brows pinched together. "Are you sure you know how?"

Her slight Irish lilt had a musical tone. He hadn't had occasion to speak to her before now. But Matt didn't need her asking questions. If Collin caught wind Matt had been poking around, he might get suspicious. He needed a distraction.

"I'm Matt." He stuck out his hand and stepped closer.

She hugged herself tighter, her eyes flashing. He froze mid-step, dropped his hand. Up close, her pallor struck him. Her arms were clamped not in anger but to hold herself steady. Memory of the night she lost Harry flickered.

"Need help unloading?" Warmth softened his tone.

"No," she muttered, turning to the wagon's rear. She slipped out of sight, though he could see her boots from beneath at the back of the wagon.

That hadn't gone the way he planned. What if she told one of her sisters he had been poking around? For now, he had no choice but to tend to the oxen, but his ears strained as they listened to the rustling of her movement, faint over the other noises of camp clamor. He slipped the pin free from the doubletree, and the nearest ox swung its head, its lip smearing slime across Matt's shirt, the stench sharp and wet. He grimaced. He was rounding the other ox, still in its traces, when a faint cry rose from Lily, sharp with distress.

He jogged to the back of the wagon, where she was wobbling beneath a swath of canvas—the tent?—its weight bowing her slender frame, her hands trembling as she fought to hold it.

"Let me help—"

"I said I don't—"

He reached out to take the weight. She jerked away from him. The canvas thudded to the ground between them, dust puffing upward in a gritty cloud.

For a moment, she stared. Then her face crumbled. But her expression went blank again just as quickly.

He was reaching out one hand, ready to help again, when an acrid scent of burning meat curled through the air. Lily's face turned a sickly green. She lurched away, bending behind the wheel, retching with hands braced on her knees, the sound harsh.

After a fractured moment, Matt jumped into action, tugging his bandana from around his neck and dunking it in the wagon's water barrel, the splash cold against his fingers. He moved to her side as she straightened, one small hand gripping the sideboard, her entire body trembling like a leaf in the wind.

"Here," he held out the damp cloth.

She eyed him warily but took it, fingers shaking as she pressed it to her mouth.

He hesitated, then asked, "Want me to fetch the nurse?"

Her chin firmed and defiance sparked in her gaze. "I'm not sick."

"You sure?"

Memory flared—Elsie's pale face outside their New York City tenement, whispering, "It'll be months before the baby comes."

Heat flushed Matt's cheeks unbidden. That was a memory he hadn't thought about in years.

He cleared his throat. "Your other sister then?" Stella would be able to help.

"No. Just leave me be." She snapped the words, sharp with finality, and turned away. He stepped back, swallowing the urge to mention his bandanna still clutched in her hand. The second ox waited, and he freed its pin from the tongue. He followed the two oxen away from the wagon, hooves thudding softly on the earth. He left Lily to do what she wished. When he glanced back, she was standing over the pile of canvas. Again, for a moment, she reminded him of Elsie.

Matt had lost touch with her after he started working for Amos.

Where was she now? Her boy must be what? Ten? Matt had been on his own by that age. Did Elsie's son look like her? Did he play jacks?

Those had been dark years, but everything had changed

when Amos had offered Matt that first job working on the docks. Now Amos wanted to make him a fixer.

Lily was his key to finding the ruby—he had a gut feeling. But tonight had shown him that getting to know her was a minefield.

Amos's deadline was looming. How quickly could he get close to Lily?

Lily stared at the tent canvas, shaky and humiliated. Her fingers trembled as she brushed a damp strand of hair from her forehead, the chill of the evening seeping through her shawl.

She hated that the cowboy had seen her in a moment of weakness. It didn't help that these past weeks her body felt completely foreign to her. The nausea, the occasional dizziness, the utter exhaustion. She hadn't known to expect any of it.

Right now, she couldn't help but feel someone was watching her. She struggled with the heavy canvas, trying to figure out which tent pole went where. She tugged at a stubborn cord, but it refused to budge. The cords seemed hopelessly tangled. Who had packed it this morning? The boys? Every time she glanced into the woods beyond the circle of wagons, the firelight thrown by flickering cook fires revealed only trees, their branches casting jagged shadows. Her breath hitched, as she squinted into the darkness, half-expecting a figure to emerge from the pines. She still couldn't shake the feeling of wrongness.

But then nothing had felt right since Harry had passed away. Perhaps she was only now registering what it meant to be truly alone.

A few minutes later, she had a wobbly excuse for a tent. The breeze played havoc with the two center poles, and she crawled inside to try to steady them. Then one of the poles fell. She ducked away, shielding her belly as it crashed.

The pole delivered a glancing blow to her shoulder. Pain flared hot and sharp, and she bit her lip to stifle a gasp, her free hand clutching her stomach protectively. The canvas fluttered down on top of her, smothering her. She shrieked in pain and frustration, knowing the material muffled the sound from their neighbors.

She'd have a bruise tomorrow for sure. Her shoulder throbbed as she shoved at the canvas, its musty scent clogging her throat. She should've taken the hired cowboy up on his offer of help. Matt, wasn't it? Maybe he was simply trying to be kind, but the offer touched on a wound still unhealed.

The first time she had spoken to Harry, he'd seen her struggling to spread the heavy canvas and jogged over to help. Before that day, she'd noticed him around camp or on horseback while he tended to the cattle. Their eyes had met more and more frequently, and she'd always lowered her gaze shyly—until the evening when Harry had struck up a short conversation after introducing himself. She could still perfectly remember the way he stood with his hat in hand, the setting sun gilding his hair.

Harry had made her heart flutter every time she looked at him. When he'd spoken to her that first time, it unleashed what felt like a flood of grasshoppers kicking around inside her stomach. This cowboy—Matt—might've been offering help out of kindness. She'd noticed pitying looks from him and the others. But his offer had only been a reminder of what she'd lost.

Now Lily clawed at the canvas, trying to find the separation where she had entered the tent.

"What on earth?" a sharp voice said from nearby.

Stella. Her older sister was the last person Lily wanted help from in this moment, but when the canvas was lifted away and Lily slipped free, taking an unencumbered breath for the first time, she did feel a bit of relief. She stumbled to her knees on the grass, gulping the cool night air, her hands splayed against the damp earth to steady herself. That relief quickly morphed into frustration as Stella parked her hands on her hips. Stella's boots crunched closer. "We've raised that tent what, seventy times since we left Independence? How is it you can't get it to stay standing?"

Lily bristled. Stella didn't think she could do anything right. She pushed to her feet, brushing dirt from her skirt with sharp, jerky motions. "It's a two-person job." It was true. She'd done fine when Paul had assisted her last night. Maddie and Jason could raise the tent in less than five minutes. Tonight, Lily had no one to help her.

Stella shook her head slightly, impatience clear in the flare of her nostrils. She bent and snatched up a corner of the canvas, her movement brisk and clipped. "Well, I'm here now."

As Stella walked around the canvas, Lily heard her mutter, "I can take time away from all the other jobs that need doing."

Lily didn't have the energy to fight. All she wanted was to crawl inside that tent and bury her head in her arms. Of course, she knew there was supper to be made and cleaned up, water for washing to be drawn. She helped with these chores nearly every day.

"How do you plan to raise the child you're carrying if you can't complete a simple task?" Stella demanded quietly as she stretched the canvas toward her.

Lily's frayed temper snapped. "I'll manage." She gave a hard yank to the canvas on her side, hard enough that it slipped out of Stella's hands.

Stella's mouth flattened into a disapproving frown. "You've always had Maddie and me to help."

"Maybe so, but I'm a grown woman now. I can manage on my own just fine," Lily said.

Stella picked up the tent and gave it a tug, but Lily hung on. Stella's grip tightened, her knuckles whitening as she leaned forward, the canvas quivering between them like a battle line.

Why couldn't her sister show some kindness? Stella's words needled at Lily's worst fears. She didn't know anything about being a mother. Her own mother—Stella's too—had died when Lily had been a small child. Lily knew how to keep a house in the city, but if Oregon was anything like this wild land surrounding them, there were so many things to be afraid of, so many things to make life difficult.

"You can barely start a fire," Stella countered. She jabbed a finger toward the nearest cook fire, its embers spitting faintly as a log shifted. "Have you ever chopped firewood before? What about milking a cow? Fetching eggs from beneath the grouchy hen?"

It was on the tip of Lily's tongue to point out that Stella didn't know how to do those things either. They'd grown up together in a tiny tenement apartment in Dublin. When they had money for it, they'd gotten their eggs from a grocer and milk from a milkman. "I didn't ask for your help, did I?" Lily said.

Stella bristled at her words. Her shoulders squared.

But Lily wasn't finished. She met Stella's gaze head-on. "You've got your own life all figured out, haven't you? A fine husband in Collin, plans for a house and a homestead, I'm sure." Lily lifted her chin. "Well, I've got my own plans."

Stella's eyes narrowed. "And what are they?"

"I don't need to share them with a bossy, overbearing sister like you. I'll pull my weight until we reach Oregon, but then I'll go my own way." Lily turned sharply, her skirt flaring as she bent to scoop up a stick from the ground.

"You can't—"

The breeze drifted in their direction again, drawing with it the scent of burning meat. Lily's stomach lurched. She pressed the handkerchief against her mouth, as bile rose in her throat. Stella had gone pale—did the scent bother her like it did Lily? Stella's hand hovered near her lips, trembling slightly as she turned her face into the wind, her skin blanching in the flickering light.

Lily suddenly realized she'd kept the cowboy's handkerchief.

Lily's gaze clashed with Stella's over the tent. Lily's pulse thudded in her ears as she stared into her sister's shadowed eyes. In another time, another situation, perhaps they would've bonded over a shared suffering. But Stella's expression shifted to something hard, her jaw clenching as she dropped her hand and straightened, turning her back with a rustle of skirts.

Lily tossed the stick toward the fire pit, her movements jerky as she fought the nausea clawing at her gut. She'd build the fire for cooking their supper and do her best to pretend her sister wasn't there.

Chapter Three

MATT RODE on horseback through the narrow valley. This climb was not steep, but so narrow that the cattle had to be driven right alongside the wagons. The cattle stretched out in a sinuous, restless line, their hooves churning the rocky earth. The valley's walls loomed like silent sentinels, their craggy faces streaked with frost that glinted faintly in the weak sunlight. A sharp wind funneled through the pass, carrying the faint tang of pine and the distant rumble of a creek hidden beyond the rise.

Farther back, Rusty rode alongside a pioneer on his horse, the old preacher's voice drifting in snippets— "Ninety-nine sheep, one lost." The pioneer had his hat tipped low as if to shield himself from the sermon.

Collin trailed even farther back, reins loose in his grip as he scanned the cattle and kept an eye on the family wagon.

But the person who kept hold of his attention was just ahead of him. Lily, minding the oxen, in conversation with an older woman whose husband was tending a milk cow and baby calf.

For the past three days, Matt had looked for any reason to talk to Lily or to visit their wagon. But with no luck.

The rocky terrain, uphill and downhill, meant the men had to watch the cattle closely from dawn to dusk. Each mile crawled by, a torturous slog through jagged trails and icy gusts that lashed at Matt's face, his awareness of Amos's deadline twisting his frustration into a tight, unyielding knot.

There was something unsettling about this valley. On the other side of the wagons, gray patches spotted the ground. Maybe mud? He couldn't figure it out.

The cattle in Matt's bunch of the herd were behaving for now. And the older woman Lily had been talking to moved off. This might be his only chance today to talk with Lily.

He nudged his horse with his knees, the leather creaking under his weight as he leaned forward, eyes fixed on her slight figure ahead. He moved away from the herd and rode several paces until he neared Lily. Then he slid from the saddle. His boots hit the rocky ground with a dull thud. He took his horse's reins in hand.

Lily glanced up at his approach, her expression guarded. He swept his hat off his head, and ran a gloved hand through his sweat-damp hair, aware of the trail grime clinging to every inch of him. He dug in his pocket, fingers brushing the empty space where his handkerchief should've been, only then realizing she still had it.

"I thought I should check on you," he said.

Her brows bunched together. She glanced toward the oxen, giving him her profile. "Why?"

He'd worked on the docks of New York Harbor for nearly ten years. Sometimes he had to tell a fib or grease the way for port authorities to look the other direction when Amos got a shipment he didn't want the law to know about. Matt was good at doing what needed done. But in the face of her pointed question, he blurted the first thing that came to mind. "Because it's the right thing to do." He stepped closer, the reins slipping slightly in his grip.

She still didn't look directly at him.

He rubbed the back of his neck. "Is there anything I can do for you?"

Her chin came up. She wrapped her arms over her middle, hugging her shawl close. "I'm not sure why you'd bother. You've no duty to me."

"Harry was a friend." A pang of guilt twisted in his gut at the white lie.

For a moment, her eyes widened. She seemed so vulnerable in that moment. Her lips parted slightly, a soft breath escaping as she tilted her head skyward.

Then he noticed the tiny snowflakes falling through the air, dusting her hair.

She glanced around in wonder, reaching out a tentative hand and catching a flake on her fingertip. "It's beautiful," she murmured.

Why couldn't he stop looking at her? He swallowed hard, his throat dry as the snow clung to her lashes, her face softening for a fleeting moment. She huddled into her shawl.

Her shoulders hunched, and she tucked her hands beneath the wool, shivering as the wind whistled past.

He tried to pull his focus back to the job—to the wagon, its canvas swaying slightly in the rising wind. To the ruby he'd been tasked to recover. He forced his gaze away from her and squinted at the Fairfax wagon, its bent hoop rattling faintly. "You need help minding the oxen?"

Her eyes flashed once more. "I'm not a child needing a minder."

He'd said the wrong thing. Again.

Beyond the wagons, the valley floor stretched long, a patchwork of frost-kissed grass and jagged stones that gleamed wetly under the gray sky. The air hung heavy with the musk of cattle and the faint, sour whiff of those mysterious gray patches, their edges glinting like wet slate.

Up ahead, the cow the man was tending with a long stick reached the edge of one of those gray patches. Instantly, its hoof sank as if into water. The bovine stumbled, the momentum pushing it farther into the gray patch, until all four hooves were covered in the muck. The animal made a blowing sound and tried to break free of the sludge. But the gray goo engulfed the animal with a greedy, sucking grip, as swift as Matt's next breath.

"Oh no!" Lily's hand flew to her mouth, her shawl slipping as she took a faltering step forward.

Her gasp into the quiet galvanized him. He suddenly imagined a wagon sinking into that pool of sludge. Her wagon. Then the ruby would be lost forever.

"Keep the wagons far away."

Those in front had missed the gray pools, but if the wagons behind took a curving route, they could sink right into it.

He grabbed the reins of his horse and tugged as he jogged toward the man staring at his sinking cow. His horse snorted, hooves clattering on the stones as he brought the beast along. He quickly passed the woman now guiding the oxen for her wagon. He was aware that Lily had followed him.

The sludge, now at the cow's belly, barely rippled with her thrashing. Her calf stood bawling nearby. The man waded in knee-deep. His arms flailed as he grabbed for the cow's shoulder. The man's hat tumbled into the muck as he lunged, his voice raw with desperation. "We need her!" he shouted.

A glance over his shoulder showed that the Fairfax oxen had veered out of the line and were moving toward other gray pools. Matt's heart lurched.

"Get back," Matt ordered Lily, grabbing a rope from his saddle. His fingers fumbled as he yanked it free, the coarse fibers snagging on his glove. He wasn't the best at throwing a loop, but that cow wasn't too far away.

The man's voice broke, panic rising as the sludge gripped his legs. He thrashed, his hands clawing at the air, mud splattering as he sank deeper. "Help me!" he cried.

Matt let the rope fly, his arm arcing wide. Held his breath until it looped the cow's neck. One part done. He glanced at the wagon as he tied the rope to his saddle horn with a quick, deft knot. The conveyance was still veering out of the line, but someone on horseback was coming fast, hopefully to rescue it.

He pulled the rope taut against the straining cow and patted the horse's shoulder to back it up. The horse snorted, hooves scraping the earth. But the cow was good and stuck. He snatched a second coil, shook it loose, intending to toss it as well, but Lily had waded in, her skirts dragging behind her as she reached for the man, her arms outstretched.

The old man grabbed her in his terror, yanking hard. She stumbled deeper, his weight pulling her down. The man lunged. Then he scrambled onto the solid ground at Matt's feet, his boots slipping as he clawed his way up. Mud streaked his trousers as he scrambled to safety.

But Lily hadn't regained her footing from his tug. She floundered, sludge swallowing her boots.

Her gasp cut sharp in the snowy air.

Lily never expected Ezra to drag her into the quicksand-like mud. It was clear that panic had overtaken him. Now the bawling calf and her own heartbeat in her ears were all she could hear. The icy sludge clutched at her legs with a relentless, chilling pull, tightening its grip with each shuddering breath she drew, though Lily knew that was silly. Terror gripped her as she tried to tug her feet free only to sink another inch deeper, the mud slurping greedily at her boots with a wet, insatiable hunger. Even her dress felt as if it was dragging her down, eager for the mud to swallow her.

She looked at Matt, but he had glanced over his shoulder. Then she saw her wagon veering wildly. When he looked back at her, his mouth had settled into a grim line. He reached for her, his hand closing around hers, firm and warm, even though hers was slick with mud. "I've got you!"

Her muddy fingers slipped, a gasp edging from her mouth. Horror in her throat, she noticed the muscles of his arm straining beneath his sleeve.

"There's no—I can't feel the bottom," she stammered. In her peripheral vision, she saw the cow a few feet away, now neck-deep in the muck. Its eyes were wild. His horse had held steady with the rope but couldn't seem to pull the cow out.

Matt's jaw clenched tight, determination etched deep in his brown eyes. "Stay still," he said, shifting his weight to try and pull her free. Panic surged inside her. This mud was a grave she didn't want to sink into.

"The more you struggle, the faster you'll sink," he warned.

It took every ounce of her will power to be still. Her breath turned shallow and ragged as she fought against the despair roaring through her veins. The other wagons kept rolling, trying to stay away from the mud. Someone had stopped Stella's wagon.

Matt's gaze flicked to his horse. "Back!" he ordered. The animal snorted, hooves pawing the earth. Ezra shouted from somewhere nearby. The calf's bawling had grown muted.

"She's too deep," Matt growled. He shot a panicked look to the cow, only its snout above the surface.

Desperation burned in her chest, and Lily's voice shook. "Get me out—please!"

Ezra muttered something, his words lost to the roar in her ears.

"No!" Matt snapped at him.

Matt still held onto her arm with one hand. In the other, a flash of silver gleamed in the sunlight. He lifted it and sliced the rope with his knife, the blade clattering to the bank with a dull thud. Matt grasped the frayed end, still attached to the horse, and wound it around his hand. He gripped so hard that his knuckles went white.

He clucked to the horse, who stepped backward. With Matt linking her and the horse, her feet moved, gaining an inch of freedom from the muck, just as she saw the cow's nose vanish completely beneath the surface.

She closed her eyes. Matt let go of her hand. This was it. She was a goner.

Then a strong arm clutched her middle, holding firm and steady. Her eyes flew open. She put her arms around his shoulders, clinging tight as one boot tore from the mud with a wet suck. One more step from the horse, one more yank, and they both collapsed on the bank, their breathing ragged. She clawed her fingers into the solid, frost-kissed earth beneath her, lying on her side, gasping for air.

She was still tucked close to Matt, his chest rising and falling beneath her cheek. Mud streaked his slicker and her skirts. He gently eased her back and sat up with a groan. But his hand was steady as he brushed her hair from her face.

Ezra's shouts rang indistinct from where he stood a few

feet away. Lily followed Matt's gaze— the pool's surface lay flat now, a smooth, gray sheen marred only by two sluggish bubbles that burst with a hollow, mournful pop. The cow was gone, swallowed by the earth's greedy maw.

She looked to Stella's wagon. The cowboy called Lucky had intervened, keeping the Fairfax wagon from heading into the mud. As he guided it back into line, he exchanged a glance with Matt. Was he making sure they were all right?

Matt helped her to her feet. Ezra loomed close, face red with fury. "That milk cow fed my family. You had no right to cut that rope!" he roared, jabbing a finger at Matt.

"You pulled Lily into that mess," Matt shot back. Mud covered his boots and the bottom of his pant legs. "She could've been killed."

The truth clung to her, and she shook. If she closed her eyes, she could still feel the muddy substance pulling at her, her clothes weighing her down.

She turned her face away, emotions swirling.

Neither man seemed to notice that the calf had attempted to follow its mama, its knobby knees sinking into the sludge near the pool's edge. Its pitiful bawl pierced the air like a child's cry.

"Ezra. Matt." Her fading terror made her voice weak. Neither one seemed to hear as they stood toe-to-toe, arguing. Lucky was still yards away, minding the wagon that she was supposed to be tending. She couldn't wade in again. But she knew how quickly that calf could disappear beneath the surface. A thick branch lay twenty feet off in the scrub. She darted for the branch, the mud on her skirt clinging like a heavy shroud, slowing her steps. She dragged it back, the weight bowing her knees as she hauled it to the pool's edge.

She hadn't thought this through—the calf couldn't grab hold.

Bending low, she crawled onto the branch, its jagged edges biting her knees through her muddy skirts. Her balance teetered as she clutched the rough wood. She couldn't look at the sludge so she kept her eyes fixed on the white patch down the middle of the calf's face. Its hide quivered as it sank lower.

"Come along, you." She reached for the calf.

"Lily!" Matt's shout rang sharp behind her.

She rose to her knees, put her arms awkwardly around the calf's middle, and heaved with all her might. Mud sucked loudly as a hoof broke free. She stumbled back on the branch, the extra weight tipping her—

Suddenly, Matt's wide shoulder braced her. One strong arm steadied her back, the other caught the calf's bulk. Matt's grunt was warm against her ear as he steadied her on firm ground. He helped her lower the calf to solid ground, its legs trembling but unharmed.

He stared into her face, his eyes deep and unreadable. "That was—"

"Foolish. So it was." Her chin lifted, fear still throbbing through her veins.

"Brave."

The word surprised her and a startled silence swelled between them.

Ezra hovered closer. Matt turned, put his shoulder

between the man and Lily, forcing Ezra back a step. "She just saved your calf."

"What good is that beast with no mama to feed it? It might as well have died."

Ezra's words, sharp and deep, made her eyes sting with tears. Matt said something she couldn't make out, and Ezra strode away. She stood trembling, taking stock—her limbs shaky from the ordeal, skirts and arms caked in layers of drying mud. Streaks of it likely smeared across her face. Her hair was probably tangled.

Matt stood at her side, a streak of mud on his jaw. He rubbed the back of his neck with one hand. For one moment, she recalled the memory of his arm around her. What was wrong with her? It had to be the fright. She stared at the calf because it was easier than looking at the man.

"He doesn't want her," Matt said.

"Poor dear," she murmured. The calf was awfully tiny.

"I suppose she's yours now."

"Ezra's right," she said. "This wee one has no mother. What do I know about its needs? I grew up in the city. I don't know animals. I don't know about plowing fields or chopping wood for a fire. I can't even mix flour proper for bread." She took a broken breath. Stella's words from the other night battered her anew, her sister's doubts echoing Lily's own fears. She felt panic rising like before.

Matt angled toward her, his hand clasping her elbow. She started. He must've seen the shock in her expression because he dropped his hand, and his brows drew together, as if he were surprised he had reached out for her.

"You saved her. She'll give you milk for your little one once she's grown a bit. That's something to start with."

His words, or maybe the shock of his touch, steadied her. Ezra had stomped off in a temper. It didn't mean he wouldn't change his mind about wanting the calf. She would need to ask Hollis to be sure she could keep it.

Matt watched her, steady and unflinching. "You'll figure a way to care for her." His certainty both steadied her and twisted her gut. Something flickered between them, but it wasn't friendship. Not yet.

Chapter Four

LILY TUGGED her shawl tighter around her shoulders as the wind sighed softly, a mournful whisper threading through the narrow mountain pass. Evening had fallen. The snow had stopped as quickly as it had begun. She'd found time for a quick wash-up with a bucket and a rag, but there was no creek where she could fully get clean tonight after the wagons had circled up. The clouds draped low over the mountaintop, heavy and brooding, bringing an eerie stillness. The air carried a definite chill, as if the snow could start falling again any moment.

The corner of camp Stella and Maddie had set up, the family campfire between the two wagons, was quiet. Men had been called to a meeting by Hollis. Lily had fought off a nauseated feeling since the near disaster by the muddy pools. The fire crackled from nearby.

Right now, she was trying to feed little Blossom. Someone said the calf had grown more listless as the afternoon had worn on. Lily tried to tempt her by tipping the wooden bucket to show her the milk inside. Blossom butted her head into the bucket and nearly toppled it from Lily's hands. She had traded a very dear sack of flour for the fresh milk from a neighbor's milk cow. She hadn't told Stella about the trade. Her sister had been angry enough about Lily keeping the calf. The momentary hope that she had felt after Matt's encouraging words was fading now, almost gone.

"Why won't you eat?"

If the calf didn't eat, it wouldn't survive.

Lily slipped a hand to her stomach, her thoughts on her own baby. Did the calf grieve for its mama? That was a fanciful idea. Lily's baby would grow up without a father. She thought of Harry. Her memories were so few, some already fleeting. She'd already forgotten his laugh. What would she tell her little girl or little boy if they asked about their father? A tear slipped free, and she quickly brushed it from her cheeks.

Children's voices in conversation met her ears, and she recognized Paul and Alex as they jogged from the camp center, the rocky ground crunching under their boots like brittle bones. Paul's knit hat was pulled low. The boys beelined for Lily—no, for Blossom.

"Did she eat yet?" Alex called out.

Paul nudged him, and Alex looked chagrined for a moment.

Alex dropped to his knees beside the calf, reaching out

both hands to pet her. His scarf slipped down around his neck as he grinned.

"I couldn't get her to suck on the rag," Lily admitted. The rag dipped in milk had been Paul's idea, something he'd seen his father do once with an abandoned lamb.

Alex's mouth set in a determined line.

"Do you mind if we try?" Paul asked.

Grief still swamping her, she gave over the bucket and the rag and moved to stand by the fire, leaving the boys with Blossom.

Only a few moments later, Paul cautioned Alex, "Careful with the bucket." Paul teased Blossom's furry lips with the milk-soaked rag. The calf tugged and sucked. Both boys' faces lit up.

"Keep going," Alex whispered.

But their muted excitement didn't touch her. Everything felt hopeless.

How was Lily to take care of a child if she couldn't care for an animal?

"Can we take Blossom over to see Jenny?" Alex turned a pleading gaze on Lily.

"We'll bring her right back," Paul promised as he rose, brushing dust from his knees.

Lily agreed and watched them trudge off with Blossom, beckoning her with smiles.

Lily squatted to stoke the fire. Stella would be back soon —she'd left Duncan, her big black stallion, tied off on the wagon parked nearby. An awful twist churned Lily's gut.

Stella was right. Lily didn't have any business trying to take care of that calf.

A shadow moved in her peripheral vision—Stella, back already? Lily turned her head and stifled a gasp as her breath caught like a shard of ice in her throat.

Irene stood in the shadows beside the wagon. Irene, who had attacked Stella with a knife and run away weeks ago. The older woman hovered, not stepping into the firelight. A ripped and torn shawl was knotted over her chest, her dress's hem tattered. It looked like it hadn't been washed in weeks. Lily opened her mouth to shout, but Irene waved a hand— or rather, the revolver in it. She pointed the gun right at Lily, whose breath froze in her chest.

"Come here, Stella," Irene ordered, voice low and rough. Her gun wobbled off-kilter—maybe Irene didn't know how to use it.

"It's me, Lily." Lily couldn't look away from the gun.

Stella had given a detailed description of shooting her first deer on this journey, including the ease of a bullet cutting through flesh, how quickly the animal bled out. What if Irene shot her? Should she run now?

As if reading Lily's thoughts, Irene pointed the gun directly at Lily's midsection, her wild eyes searching all over the camp. Her cheeks were gaunt since Lily had seen her last.

"Where—where did you come from?" Lily breathed.

"Thought you drove me off, didn't you?" Irene's hand trembled with fury, the gun wavering. "I want my ruby. Give it to me."

"I—I don't have it," Lily stammered. She glanced

around quickly. There was no one nearby to see that she needed help. For one brief moment, she was glad the boys had left.

"Liar!" Irene spat. She stepped closer, then shrank back into the shadows. She seemed out of it, confused.

"I'm not lying—Stella lost it," Lily said, the lie bitter on her tongue. Stella *had* lost the jewel, but she'd found it several days later hidden beneath a broken panel in the wagon.

"You're Stella." Irene shook her head with a violent jerk. Her eyes darted around wildly. "You didn't lose it. You hid it."

Voices carried. Were the boys coming back? Lily searched for something she might use as a weapon. A cooking pot? A branch from the fire? In her moment of distraction, Irene closed the gap between them, seizing Lily's arm in her bony grip. She jabbed the revolver into the tender part of Lily's side.

Lily gasped as ice flowed through her veins.

"Quiet," Irene muttered, her breath fanning hot against Lily's cheek.

At this range, it would be impossible for her to miss if that gun went off.

"Get me the jewel," Irene demanded.

"I can't," Lily whispered. "Stella lost it." Lily prayed forgiveness for the lie even as her mind spun—where had Stella stashed the jewel?

"I don't believe you," Irene growled, yanking Lily's arm. "If Stella's got the jewel then you're coming with me."

Lily struggled, but Irene jabbed the revolver harder into her side. Pain bloomed beneath her ribs.

"I will shoot you," Irene hissed, breath ragged. "Now come on."

Irene shoved her around the wagon and toward Duncan. Lily's boot slipped against the ground, fear for her baby choking her. She couldn't fight—not with a gun pressed against her and Irene so unfocused and confused and fearful. Snow began to fall, a thick curtain of soft flakes veiling the camp in an ominous hush.

Duncan stamped, snorting as they neared, his reins pulling taut between him and the wagon.

"Get on," Irene ordered. "I'm done walking. Been chasing the company, and I'm starving."

Was Irene the one who had been following the company? Hollis and the other leaders had claimed they'd seen a man—or had it been a horse? Lily couldn't remember in this terrifying moment.

"I'm no horsewoman," Lily said.

"Get up on him." Another jab, sharp against her side.

Tears stung Lily's eyes as she fumbled her foot into the stirrup, arms trembling.

"I ain't joking—I'll shoot you," Irene snarled.

Lily jumped from the ground and hauled herself awkwardly into the saddle, the leather creaking beneath her weight. Irene untangled the reins and tossed them up. They slapped Lily's cheek, the leather stinging against her cold skin.

Irene scrambled onto Duncan's back, the horse shying

with a sidestep. He was a difficult animal; only Stella could ride him with any measure of success.

Irene's bony arm snaked around Lily's middle, nearly unseating her. The grip was iron-tight.

"Get moving," Irene commanded, the revolver jabbing once more.

"Where—?" Snow blurred Lily's sight, cloaking the world in a disorienting white shroud.

"Just go," Irene snapped, her breaths coming quick and fast.

Lily nudged Duncan into motion. Thankfully, he walked instead of rearing up in protest at the two riders who were unaccustomed to being on his back. Lily squinted, looking for any kind of help through the falling snow.

There was nothing.

No one.

* * *

Snow stung Matt's cheeks, the wind slicing sharp and spiteful against his exposed skin. He'd left the cowboy camp moments ago, the faint glow of their tiny fire flickering behind him like a fading ember. Rusty had been lecturing Gerry while the others played cards.

A cut in the jagged slope cradled the herd, a small meadow where cattle clumped together, their breath steaming in the frigid air. Matt's boots crunched through the deepening drift. He had to figure out a way to get into that wagon, to search for the ruby. He'd decided to use the calf as his excuse, aware of time ticking away.

The blowing snow made it harder to identify the Fairfax wagon, even with its bent rear hoop, but he kept searching among the circled wagons. For a moment, he replayed those moments when Lily had stood on the bank of that patch of quicksand, covered in mud. The vulnerable look in her eyes showed just how much she trusted him. Now he was using the friendship he'd engineered to take advantage of her.

It made something ugly twist inside him. He tried to ignore it.

He'd worked for Amos for years. He'd lied to a lot of different men, snuck around behind their backs. He hadn't seen anything wrong with it, so why was it bothering him that Lily might be hurt?

The wagons warped into view through the snow. As he neared, he saw Duncan, Stella's horse, dancing away from the wagon, hooves hitting the ground with a restless thud. Two figures sat atop the horse.

Lily's face stood out stark against the snow. What was she doing on that horse? He squinted. The second rider hunched low, shrinking as if she wanted to vanish in Lily's shadow.

But dark hair spilled from a tattered shawl, and he knew it wasn't Stella.

Lily's head turned. Had she called for help? Or was the wind playing tricks on his ears?

The snow muted all the sounds.

He sent a fleeting glance to her wagon. Their campsite

was empty. This was his chance. For one brief moment, the snow lifted, and he saw her face, the clear expression of fear etching her features.

Something was wrong.

But this was his chance.

A beat of worry for Lily tugged him forward. He jogged after the horse, boots kicking through the dusting of snow. The stallion's black form cut a path through the swirling flakes. Why leave camp in a building storm? Dread bloomed beneath his ribs, and he broke into a run, stumbling as his boot struck a buried rock.

As Matt drew closer, the horse angled down into a ravine well past the company's camp. Instinct had his hand brushing the revolver at his hip as he slowed to peer over the edge.

No one had noticed him.

He scrambled over the ravine's lip, saw what might be a deer trail winding along the steep descent, barely discernible through the blowing snow. The horse was picking its way down the trail away from him. Matt moved as quickly as he could. But then, for one jagged moment, the horse turned on a switchback.

Matt tried to duck—too late.

A shout rose—Lily's voice, sharp with fear. A gunshot cracked, echoing off the ravine's walls. Dirt spat five feet to his left.

The stallion reared with a whinny. Both women tumbled to the ground with shrieks.

"Help!" Lily cried.

Who made the shot? Not Lily. Who was with her?

Matt scrambled down the incline, branches snagging his trousers and gloves as he slid. The other rider hadn't gotten up. She writhed on the ground while the horse raced off into the snow and growing dark.

Lily scrambled away from where she'd landed—angling right toward the place where Matt would meet her. Another shot rang out. Snow kicked up.

Matt dropped low, staying as close to the ground as he could, his heart racing beneath his ribs. He'd almost reached Lily. What if whoever was aiming that gun found her first?

A wild idea gripped him. He whistled sharp, as Stella once had.

Silence.

The sound of a gun being cocked.

His hand reached out and tangled with Lily's—

Hoofbeats were the only warning as the black stallion raced up the hill. The woman stumbled back, nearly trampled.

Matt caught Lily against his side. She was shaking so badly—how was she even standing upright?

"Come on," he said. They moved as quickly as she could manage; she seemed to be limping. It was an awkward half-run, stumbling through the snowy, craggy ravine. He meant to angle up the hill, where they could circle around and get back to camp, but in the dark, his direction must have been off. They staggered into a wash, the ground flattening into an icy, treacherous expanse at the ravine's bottom.

"Hold on a second," he said. He strained his ears over

the sound of both of them breathing hard. There was no noise of pursuit.

"I don't hear her—do you?" he asked.

"No," she whispered, her voice small against the wind. She was huddled into herself, and he felt her take a shaky breath. "I thought she was going to shoot me." The last word broke on a quiet sob that she stifled.

Some long-buried instinct made Matt tighten his arm around her back. She must've taken it for comfort because she turned into him, pressing closer as her shoulders shook silently.

"She held a gun on you?" he asked. That's why Lily had been on the back of that horse. Because she'd been coerced.

He tried to focus on that, not Lily's fine hair brushing the underside of his jaw or the warmth of her breath on the cold skin of his neck. "Did you hurt your leg?" he asked.

She nodded, her head bumping his chin. "Twisted my ankle coming off the horse." She took another jittery breath. "She might've killed me if you hadn't come."

Her words, along with the trust she showed by burrowing into him, struck Matt like a blow. He'd come up with the idea of befriending her, but it had been a fluke that he'd followed her away from camp. He wasn't her friend. That ugly feeling he'd felt when he approached her wagon rose inside him to choke off his breath. He cleared his throat.

"We need to find someplace to shelter for the night. I'm afraid to try and climb back up to camp without a lantern." He didn't mention that a lantern would make them more visible. She moved a step away in the dark but then went still. Was she afraid to be out here with him?

"And we don't know if that woman—"

"Irene." The word came out small. The name struck a chord. Where did he know it from?

"Irene," he echoed. "We don't know where Irene's gone. If she's waiting somewhere between here and camp, she might shoot at us again."

"Won't we freeze out here?" A faint rustle, as if she'd raised her arm to brush her face—brush the tears away? "No blankets, no food. Can we make a fire?"

"The glow would point her right to us. She might even smell the smoke." It had grown so dark. The world had dissolved into a swirling abyss of snow and shadow, leaving him blind to any shelter. But they couldn't just stand in the blowing snow.

"Come on." He wrapped one hand around hers and kept the other outstretched in front of him, taking slow, careful steps and feeling the ground before each one to make sure it wasn't going to fall away beneath him. "Why did this Irene grab you?" he asked.

She hesitated. "We met her in New York City. She helped us out of a...tight spot. And then she came west with us."

His heart thrummed. That's where he knew the name. She worked for Amos. Or was there more?

Lily stumbled, and he reacted, steadying her and keeping her upright.

"She turned on us," Lily's words faltered, and her breath shuddered out. "She was really scared someone was coming after us." The way she hesitated as she spoke and the holes in her story made him question everything. Had Irene helped them steal the ruby? She was rumored to have been a former sweetheart of Amos's. Why hadn't he mentioned that she had been a part of the theft?

"We left her behind at one of the forts weeks ago."

He processed this new information as his hand brushed what seemed like a rock wall. It would provide some shelter from the wind. In fact, he already felt it blocking the wind. If they huddled together—they might make it.

"We brushed against a small tree a few yards back," he said. "Stay here, and I'll cut some branches to cover us."

The mountains loomed darker than the sky. His mind was spinning with everything that Lily had just told him. Irene was after the ruby. She was desperate enough to sneak into camp and use a gun to get Lily to give it to her. An urgency rose inside Matt. He hadn't known there was competition out here. That meant he needed to find the ruby as soon as possible and make tracks back to New York City.

* * *

Rob Braddock knelt beside a wagon wheel, his breath puffing white in the crisp night air, the cold gnawing through his gloves as he pounded the wooden spoke into place on the wheel. Its metal rim creaked in the cold. Fine snowflakes caught in his eyelashes, and the chill wind slipped down his collar. For a moment, he wished he was sitting beside the fire in the great room of his grandfather's house. The massive stone fireplace warmed several rooms in the mansion, and some of Rob's fondest memories involved curling up on a rug before that fire with a book when he was a kid.

He reminded himself again that this journey would be worth it. The cold, the weariness. All of it. Once he won Alice back.

Caleb Carter shifted where he held the wheel steady for Rob and adjusted his grip. The pioneer was maybe a decade older than Rob and had a family to look after. He was one of the handful of folks who had befriended him on this trip. Most were loyal to the Spencer and Mason families.

Rob gave the spoke one final tap. He wiped his forehead with the back of his glove. "I think that's it."

He stood and rolled his shoulders, watching as Caleb raised his arms over his head in a stretch. Rob flexed his hands, fingers stiff and numb from the cold.

"Happy to help," Caleb said. He clapped his hands together, a muffled thud echoing as he blew into them, his breath clouding in the dim light. "Especially since you shared your venison with us last week."

Rob nodded, moving to put away the hammer inside the wagon but Caleb wasn't done. "Lots of city folk don't know how to repair these wagons."

Rob flushed and hoped it wasn't visible in the faint flicker of firelight from yards away. Grandfather had ensured he had the very best education—tutors from France and England. He knew how to manage the powder mill after years of working at his grandfather's side. Just because Rob didn't know how to tinker with a wagon wheel didn't mean he wasn't capable of completing the plans he had made before he left the East. He was going to make this adventure a success, and not just for men like Caleb. He squared his shoulders as a gust rattled the wagon's canvas behind him.

"I'm going to start a mill once we reach the Willamette Valley. I've got funds to pay workers."

Even in the faint light, Rob saw Caleb's eyes light up. He had three kids and another one on the way. His two oldest had been barefoot the last time Rob had seen them. He was making do with a wagon that must've been years old when it left Independence and had been repaired over and over. People like Caleb had come west with a dream but no real plan.

"I could use a man like you to help me get the mill up and running."

A voice turned Caleb's head. He squinted into the darkness toward his wagon. "I want to hear more about your mill," he said before he trudged off through the gathering snowdrift. His figure faded into the gloom.

Distant pines groaned against the wind but satisfaction surged inside Rob. He knew he could talk Caleb into seeing things his way. He surveyed the wagon, now dusted with snow. He brushed a hand over the wheel, flakes scattering as his fingers traced the cold, rough wood. Most nights he hadn't bothered to pitch a tent. He'd just slept underneath the wagon. But the snow tonight would make curling up in a bedroll with no shelter miserable.

That fire in Grandfather's fireplace flickered through his memory again. He closed his eyes for a heartbeat, the imagined warmth warring with the chill seeping through his coat.

Movement snagged his gaze—Alice Spencer striding past, her arms laden with a bundle of blankets. His heart leaped, even though her chin was turned stiffly away. Had she been close enough to overhear? He took a step toward her, snow squeaking underfoot.

"You need any help?" he called out. His voice cracked slightly, and he cleared his throat, shoving his hands into his pockets.

Her eyes flicked to him, then past where Caleb had disappeared into the darkness.

"I'm fine." The way she walked made it clear she had no intention of stopping.

He couldn't resist calling out after her again. "Maybe Collin will come work for me."

Before everything that had happened in New Jersey, he and the middle Spencer brother had had a good work relationship.

Alice stopped, her chin came up, and her eyes flashed. Her lips pressed into a thin line. "I don't have a care about your plans—I'm certain you'll run whatever business you create in the same way your grandfather would." Her voice sliced through the night air, just as cold. "My brother would rather starve than work for a man of questionable ethics."

Anger flared. Rob's hands balled into fists inside his pockets. Her brother Coop had nearly burnt down Grandfather's mills.

She took a step closer, her boots crunching in the traces of snow. She looked around, almost as if she was ashamed to be caught talking to him.

His temper swelled brighter. "My mill will be run with precision. It will be a great success. I've calculated how much it will earn." Rob wanted to build something real, something that belonged to himself, not to Grandfather.

The wind tugged her coat, whipping a strand of dark blonde hair across her face. She brushed it back with an impatient flick, and her lips curled.

"You don't think I can do it?"

"I think you'll step on whoever you need to step on to accomplish your ends, just like your grandfather."

The words left him reeling.

But she wasn't done.

"You just said you'd calculate your profits—why don't you send a letter to your grandfather and ask how he made so much money? He paid workers a pittance for doing dangerous jobs." She meant her brothers. She must've been shaken by the explosion, by how close it had been to losing one of them.

He shook his head sharply, snow tumbling from his hat as he took another step. "Grandfather and I are not the same."

Her eyes flashed. She hugged the blankets tighter, her chin jutting defiantly. "I see no difference."

She blinked, must've realized how close they were standing, nearly toe-to-toe now. She backed up a step and then began to walk off, her motions quick and jerky, the blankets swaying where she clutched them to her chest. Before she could go more than a couple steps, he caught her arm, his fingers closing around her elbow.

She jerked away.

"Alice, stop. I don't want to fight with you." He stepped closer, only for her to retreat another pace.

She swallowed, eyes dark. He couldn't help but notice the snowflakes that clung to her lashes.

"I still have feelings for you." He dropped his hand to his side as he leaned toward her, his voice rough with emotion. "Strong as ever, tearing me up inside. And I know you still have feelings for me, even if you won't admit it."

Her mouth pinched as she shook her head slightly. "How could I care for a man my brothers hate? Your grandfather sent those coppers after Coop."

"And your brothers hid him away," he reminded her as angry heat surged up his neck.

"We lost everything because of you and your grandfather—our friends, our home. We had to leave and come west with nothing. My brothers will never forgive you, and neither will I." Her voice trembled as she took another step back.

And then she turned and slipped away while he floundered for an argument she would listen to. She crossed camp. Her older brother, Leo, was waiting near the Spencer wagon. Leo glared at Rob, arms crossed over his chest, his broad shoulders squared as he shifted his weight. He spoke to Alice—probably looking for a reason to come after Rob.

Rob's chest tightened as he stared at them. Alice had her back to Rob, murmuring something, her shoulders stiff.

Leo's scorn and Alice's words fueled a slow, simmering ache inside him. He turned away, trudged toward the wagon, his hands shoved deep into his pockets as the cold bit at his ears.

How could she throw away everything they'd shared? He'd come over one thousand miles intending to win her back.

She'd thrown a gauntlet.

Now all he needed to do was figure out a way to win her brothers over.

Chapter Five

LILY WOKE with her neck stiff and bent at an odd angle. For a moment, she couldn't remember where she was.

Then she registered the arm heavy around her shoulders and the warmth at her side.

Irene.

The snowstorm.

Matt.

She held her breath as she realized exactly how closely they were tucked together.

A thin band of silver light broke through the darkness behind the mountaintop that stood sentinel over them. She wasn't cold, though her exposed skin was chilled. Sometime in the night, Matt must've shed his coat because now they sat tucked as close as could be, the rock wall behind them, and his coat was spread over them like a blanket.

A very small blanket.

One of her hands rested flat on his stomach, and her head was tucked into the crook between his neck and shoulder. The tiniest of snores escaped him.

He was holding her close—even closer than Harry had done before he'd died.

Surely they had grown extremely cold in the night and had clung together for warmth. It wasn't wrong to stay alive, was it?

Still, the twist in her gut and the vague sense of guilt clogging her throat plagued her.

Her breathing must've changed, or maybe she shifted ever so slightly, because his breath caught. He went very still. And then he shifted slightly, one of his knees dropping so that his leg stretched out, foot now sticking out of their coat-blanket. But he didn't move his arm from around her shoulders.

"You all right?" The low rumble of his voice cracked with sleep.

She nodded, a sudden shyness keeping her face averted. "As well as I can be, sleeping outside in a snowstorm." She tried to straighten some of the wrinkles from her skirt, but it was a lost cause. "I never slept outdoors until we began this terrible journey."

"It's not so bad if you've got something to cover up with. Piece of canvas. Even newspaper..." He trailed off. If she wasn't mistaken, a flush was rising at his jawline.

"Do you mean you've slept out in the elements before?"

Now she was sure the red blaze in his cheeks was a blush. He scooted out from underneath the coat, stood, and brushed one hand through his hair as if agitated. "I don't remember much of my parents. They died, and I was on my own by the time I was eight years old. I didn't have a home... Sometimes I slept outside. In alleys and under bridges. You can feel some heat coming through a closed doorway behind a restaurant or cafe."

She was already missing the warmth from his body.

"I'm sorry," she said softly. "That must have been very difficult."

He glanced away, a muscle in his jaw ticking. "It was a long time ago."

How had he come to be here, a hired hand on this wagon train? Had anyone ever helped him? Had he found a home? She wanted to ask more, but she sensed he wouldn't welcome her prying.

The sky had grown lighter, the shadows fading and sun beginning to glare off the snowy surfaces. They couldn't stay out here. And Lily shouldn't huddle underneath Matt's coat any longer. She tugged her shawl tighter around her and knotted it at her middle before pushing his coat from her shoulders. "Here, you'll be wanting this back."

The wool garment twisted in her hands as Matt took a step toward her.

Something metal clinked against the dry rocks at her side.

"What's this?"

Matt suddenly squatted beside her, pushing her hand away. "Those are mine."

He slipped off his glove to pick up the small pieces.

If he hadn't just told her a part of his difficult child-hood, she might've taken offense at the sharpness in his tone.

He ducked his head for a moment and then exhaled in a gust. He opened his palm to reveal several small metal gears and delicate brass pieces. This is what had fallen from his coat pocket?

"What are they?" she asked quietly.

He cleared his throat. "Pieces of a pocket watch. I consider them a talisman." He slipped them back into an inside pocket of the coat before straightening to his full height. He swung the garment behind him to slip his arms into the sleeves. "I admired watches on a coupla well-to-do fellas when I was young. Always wanted one." His deft fingers moved to button up his coat. He slipped his glove back on. "I found one on the street. It was smashed up real good like it'd been run over by a carriage wheel. I musta been all of twelve. Figured it had fallen off some dandy. I kept the pieces. It had a real nice gold chain. Worth a pretty penny. I kept that, too. Promised myself one day I'd have a nice watch to hang on it."

She twisted her ankle this way and that, slowly. It still hurt but not like it had last night. "And did you? Get your pocket watch?"

He shook his head. "Not yet."

But the determination in his voice told her he would. Someday.

Lily reached up to grasp Matt's proffered hand, bracing herself as she pushed to her feet. A sharp twinge shot through her ankle, and she couldn't suppress a gasp as it threatened to give out beneath her.

Matt's other hand was immediately at her elbow, steadying her. "Careful now."

She nodded, heat rising to her cheeks at their closeness, her fingers still wrapped in his. The cool morning air did nothing to ease the awkwardness between them.

"Try to take a step."

She nodded. But before she'd managed to move, nausea swamped her. She clutched Matt's arm tighter, ducked her head, and swallowed against the bile rising up her throat.

His arm stayed steady around her. "What's the matter? Your ankle?"

She couldn't speak, too afraid that opening her mouth would make her lose her tenuous hold on what wanted to come up.

This time when he spoke, there was a soft note she hadn't expected. "The baby?"

She nodded slightly. He seemed to be waiting for her to say more.

"It hits me hard if I let myself get too hungry," she whispered.

They hadn't eaten supper last night. Nor did they have anything to make a meal now.

"If you can manage it, we'll head up the mountain and get back to the wagons. Get you some food."

Head still ducked, she squeezed her eyes closed as tears welled. It was supposed to be Harry here at her side. Harry helping her.

But Harry was gone. And she was forced to rely on Matt, a virtual stranger.

No, that wasn't quite right. A stranger wouldn't have come after her when Irene had taken her from camp. Wouldn't have huddled close with her all night.

"All right," Lily whispered. "Let's go."

But she hesitated, glancing around the snow-dusted landscape. The rocky outcrops and sparse trees provided plenty of hiding spots. "What if Irene is out there? Waiting for us to move."

His gaze swept around them, the movement was so familiar that she realized he'd been scanning for danger the entire time they'd been awake.

"She could be," Matt admitted, his hand moving toward the gun at his hip as if out of habit. "But she likely has limited ammunition. And this open space gives us good line of sight. We'll see her coming."

And it wasn't as if they had a choice. They couldn't stay here with no food or firewood, no weapons other than his revolver. All of a sudden, she wanted Stella. Even though they were still at odds, Stella's protective, bossy nature seemed exactly what Lily needed in this moment.

The events of the past day—Irene's surprise arrival, the snowstorm, the forced intimacy with Matt—had shaken Lily's already fragile sense of security.

As they set out, Matt kept his arm around her, supporting her weight as she limped along beside him. She kept her focus on taking each next step, yet each step sent a jolt of pain through her ankle. But she pressed on.

In her peripheral vision, she saw Matt's gaze constantly sweeping the stark landscape for any sign of danger lurking behind the snow-laden trees or jagged boulders.

* * *

Lily leaned heavily into Matt as they picked their way up the hillside. Each time she took a limping step, he caught the flicker of pain that crossed her expressive face. But any time he glanced directly at her, she masked it with a smile.

From here, he could see where they'd come down from the plateau above, the untouched wilderness marred by crushed bushes and brambles.

There was no sign of the black stallion.

Or of Irene.

Had she snuck back up to the camp? Or was she waiting somewhere out here, biding her time?

This side of the mountain was even more wild than what the company had traversed yesterday. Some part of Matt admired the wild, dangerous beauty of it. But another glance at Lily had a protective urge rising inside him. He couldn't figure it. Was it because she reminded him of Elsie? Last night, just before he'd slipped off to sleep, he'd felt an unexpected stirring of affection with Lily tucked close to his side.

In the light of morning, with the distance she was gently enforcing, any affection between them seemed ridiculous. He had a job to do. Needed to use whatever friendship was blooming between them to get it done. He couldn't afford to get further entangled with her.

She stumbled, and he caught her, barely keeping both of them upright.

"Do you need a rest?" he asked.

"I'm fine. Let's keep going." She flicked a glance at the top of the hill. There was still a lot of climbing ahead of them, but the stubborn tilt of her chin showed the fire driving her. When they started off again, her leg threatened to crumple. He did his best to unobtrusively take more of her weight.

If she intended to reach the top of that hill herself, maybe he could create a distraction from her pain.

"Do you think we'll run into any more of that quicksand?" he asked. "I never imagined something like that could be real."

"I haven't been able to stop thinking about those pits." Her brow furrowed slightly as if she was imagining them all over again. "The branch didn't sink—at least not very fast. What if something wide—like a barrel lid or a plank—could've spread the weight enough to help get that cow out?"

She took a few more agonizing steps. "I would wager a man could cross on a plank."

Matt's lips quirked. "That's a dangerous notion—even for someone as brave as you."

This time when he glanced at her, her eyes danced away shyly. She went quiet.

Matt's thoughts drifted to what he'd shared earlier, when his past had spilled out unbidden. He hadn't meant to share so much. Lily was a good listener. But it was more than that.

He'd intended to use their growing friendship as a way to find an opportunity to get the ruby. But he hadn't expected to feel the vulnerability he'd experienced when he'd told her about his early days. He didn't like to think about those dark days. Had he opened up too much?

A sharp rustle snapped from the underbrush to their right, shattering the stillness and breaking him from his thoughts.

Lily froze with a startled gasp.

His hand went to his revolver.

A deer burst out of the brush, hooves flinging snow. It darted across their path, white tail flashing, and disappeared into a grove of dense pines across the clearing.

Matt's pulse roared in his ears. Lily's fingers clenched on his coat sleeve.

There was no real danger.

"Sorry," she murmured.

"It's all right. It startled me too."

They pressed on. Was she flagging? Should he insist on a rest?

Only a few moments had passed when a shout echoed from the hilltop. Matt's head jerked up as he searched for its source.

"Lily!" Stella's voice rang clear.

There. Three figures on the ridge above, picking over the snow-dusted landscape. Stella, Collin, and Doc.

Lily must've seen them too, because her breath caught.

Collin pointed in their direction. Stella adjusted her

trajectory and stormed toward them, eyes blazing, the two men a few paces behind.

"Where have you been?" she demanded. "We found Duncan running loose—" Still approaching, her glare switched to fix on Matt. "What did you do to her?"

"Stella—" Lily started.

Matt let go of Lily as Stella moved with a burst of speed toward him. She shoved his shoulders, and he fell back a step, holding up both hands in front of him.

"We ran into trouble—"

But Stella's eyes flashed in a way that said she didn't want to listen. Not to Lily and not to him.

"Stella, stop!" Lily's cry sliced sharp. "We didn't leave camp by choice."

Collin had finally caught up to them and put out an arm to bar Stella's advance. His gaze flicked to Lily. "What happened?"

"Irene found me alone in camp," Lily said, as Doc steadied her. "She pulled her gun, demanded the ruby."

Stella snapped. "What?"

The ruby. Matt felt a flush of heat. It was the first time any of them had admitted aloud that they had it in their possession.

Doc knelt beside Lily as Stella and Collin exchanged a loaded glance.

"Twist your ankle?" the doc asked. When Lily nodded, he reached out to examine her appendage.

"She wanted the ruby," Lily went on, wincing as Jason

probed her foot carefully. "She seemed... confused. Called me Stella. When I said I didn't have it, she forced me on Duncan."

Collin was watching Matt with a narrow-eyed gaze.

"I saw her riding off with this Irene on your black," Matt offered. "Something felt wrong—so I followed them."

"Duncan threw us," Lily added, sniffling. "I hurt my ankle. Irene fired her gun. We hid, then the snow was coming too fast for us to make it back to camp..."

Stella's eyes flicked to Matt. He still couldn't decide if her expression meant apology for shoving him or anger that he was here with Lily. His shoulders straightened minutely. He wasn't the one who'd left Lily alone in camp.

"I'd have frozen without his coat," Lily murmured.

Jason stood, brushing snow from his knees. "It's not sprained, but she'll need to rest it a day or two." He eyed the climb still in front of them. "I'd rather she didn't climb this hill, though."

"We can make a litter," Matt said.

Collin moved to Lily's side. "I'll carry her." He swept Lily into his arms.

Doc fell in beside Matt as he followed Collin carrying Lily. "You injured?"

Matt shook his head, gaze flicking to Stella walking beside Collin. Her muttered words drifted to him. "We need to stop Irene before she tries worse. She's a threat to us all now."

Including Matt, who might be in the most danger of all.

He didn't know whether Irene had seen his face. It had been dark, and the blowing snow had obscured almost everything. If she'd seen him and recognized him, if she knew he worked for Amos, she might be even more desperate to get to the ruby first.

He had to find it. Fast.

Chapter Six

A FEW MINUTES after returning to camp, Matt was hunkered by the dying campfire, soaking up its warmth. He knew the bugle would blow soon; the snow hadn't been enough to keep the company stationary. He shoveled what was left of his breakfast into his mouth and watched the ten rolls of gray smoke curling upward through the crisp air. Around him, the other cowboys were gathered: Lucky cross-legged, whittling a stick; Gerry Bones lingering, his plate empty; Coop a few feet off, stretched out with arms folded behind his head resting against the weathered log, his hat tipped low over his eyes.

Matt's eyes skipped over Rusty, who'd told Matt he had prayed for him throughout the night when he hadn't come back to camp.

Collin and Leo strode toward the hired hands, tension clear in the set of their shoulders. They walked straight to Matt. Collin stood loose-limbed while Leo crossed his arms over his chest. "Which way did Irene go? Did you see tracks?"

Matt chewed slowly and then swallowed. "I told Collin everything I know. Every detail." *Where is that ruby hidden?* He kept the question behind his teeth, but it burned inside him now that he knew for sure that Stella had it. He set his empty bowl aside, the clink of tin faint against the frozen earth.

Leo's glance encompassed all the hired hands. "We want our men on watch over the company, not just the cattle. We'll keep a skeleton crew with the beasts."

"Why didn't you tell us someone would be shooting at us?" Matt asked. "I thought we were watching for bears or cougars. What are we facing here?"

Lucky glanced up from his saddlebag, curiosity evident on his face.

Gerry Bones's shoulders stiffened. His voice was gruff when he spoke. "Ain't right for a boss to keep secrets, 'specially ones that put us in danger."

Rusty was usually quiet and contemplative in meetings like this, but he spoke up now. "I didn't sign on to take a bullet. It's dangerous enough out here in the wilderness."

A murmur of discontent rippled through the men.

Coop propped up on an elbow. "Me, either."

Leo scowled at his brother, and a muscle ticked in Collin's cheek.

Neither one spoke directly to Coop.

Gerry grunted. "It's downright frightening to think there's a madwoman stalking us somewhere out there. I heard rumors about a man trailing us, but a woman's even more frightening. Never know what a skirt will do."

A man hunting the company? Matt hadn't heard that particular rumor. He'd heard tell that some men had been apprehended a few weeks out from Independence—figured it had to be Amos's hired muscle. Was it possible one of them was still out in the wilds somewhere?

Leo's gaze locked with Collin's for a moment, a silent exchange. "We'll offer extra pay for anyone who stays on."

Rusty straightened. "How much?"

Lucky muttered, "Ain't sure any amount is worth it."

Collin kept his tone calm, his stance projecting an ease that surely he didn't feel. "Anyone who doesn't want to stand guard over the womenfolk can stay with the cattle. No hard feelings."

Matt leaned forward, eyes fixed on Leo. "If someone's hunting us, what do they want?"

The fire popped, a thin wisp of smoke curling upward. Leo shifted, his gaze skittering away.

"It's a jewel, isn't it?" Matt pressed. "Lily said that's what the lady asked for."

A new murmur rippled through the men. Lucky set his whittling down. Gerry sat up, eyes sparking.

"What kind of jewel?" Rusty asked, voice sharp.

"How much is it worth?" Gerry added, leaning in.

Leo's frown carved deeper lines. "Worth enough for her to near starve while trailing us for weeks to claim it. But that's none of your concern."

Collin shot his brother a glance after the clear dismissal.

Matt rose, joints crackling from the cold and the sleepless night. When Collin gestured him aside, he followed a few steps away as the cowboys continued talking—maybe arguing—with Leo.

Stella's fury that morning still stung, especially after he'd risked his hide to save Lily. Was Collin intending to reprimand him, too?

Collin met Matt's stare straight on. "I want to thank you for what you did for Lily."

Surprise caught Matt off guard.

"If you hadn't followed her and Irene out there, hadn't stayed through that storm, who knows what might've happened."

Collin's obvious gratitude hit in a way Matt hadn't known to brace for. Throughout his childhood and teen years, he'd dodged brooms, scrabbled for scraps, slept in doorways. He'd had friends, but he had always been aware that they were as desperate as he was and would just as likely take his portion if they got a chance. Amos had given him the opportunity to get away from that hardscrabble life, but there were consequences for failure in Amos's world. It held no softness, no gratitude.

"Lily isn't like Stella or Maddie. They've always shielded her and..." Collin shook his head, swallowing whatever his next thought would've been. "It could've ended far worse."

Matt recalled Lily's quiet strength from this morning, her compassion as he had talked about his past, her grit climbing that hill with a twisted ankle. "She's stronger than you think."

Collin's eyes narrowed. There was an intensity in his stare now. "We'll be pulling out soon."

"I'd like to check on Lily," Matt said. He strode off through the camp bustle toward the Fairfax wagon.

As he approached, he spotted Lily with Maddie and Doc's boys huddled near the calf. Coop stood guard beyond the wagons now, rifle loose at his side, his back to the company and head swiveling as he kept watch. He must've been sent over by Leo. No one else lingered near.

Matt drew close as the calf butted a bucket from Lily's hands, the wooden pail clattering to the earth, milk splashing across the soil. Lily's dismay showed in the flare of her nostrils.

Alex earnestly patted Lily's arm. "At least she took some from the rag."

Lily looked up as Matt closed the short distance between them.

He recognized the pinch in her lips as frustration. "You all right?"

She smiled tightly. "She still won't drink from the bucket."

"She's too little," Alex piped up.

Paul's concerned expression mirrored Lily's.

"I'm sure you'll think of something," Matt said gently. "What about you? Did you eat?"

Alex's eyes went wide as he looked at Matt. "We heard you rescued Lily." Admiration glowed in his tone.

Matt's chest wanted to expand with pride, but that feeling was quickly followed by a twist in his gut. His intentions toward Lily weren't pure. He didn't deserve the boy's admiration.

"Maddie said we could make snow ice cream." Alex's excitement bubbled out, infectious. "Lily's gonna help. Do you wanna help too?"

Lily must've caught Matt's confusion because one corner of her lips twitched with amusement. Her nearness stirred him—the memory of her hand on his arm, her breath against his neck as they had slept.

What was wrong with him?

His voice emerged rough, and he had to clear his throat before he spoke. "Snow ice cream?"

A shadow passed through her eyes, so swiftly that he almost didn't see it—a memory of what had passed between them this morning, what she knew about him that no one else did. "If you have a few minutes to spare, we'll show you."

Lily sat on a crate and lifted the bucket that the calf had spilled. There was still a bit of milk left in the bottom.

"You get started with the treat. I'll finish with Blossom," she said. Matt followed the boys to the wagon, and she caught the glance he sent her over his shoulder—the uncertainty in his eyes surprised her. The boys handed him the biggest mixing bowl, arguing over who was going to add the cream. Matt answered them, his voice so low she couldn't make out his words.

Both boys scampered to the snow that had drifted beneath the wagon and other places, carefully cupping it in their hands to dump in the bowl. She tried to focus on what she was doing, dipping one corner of the cloth in the bucket and then offering it to Blossom, who suckled it somewhat in her mouth. After a few times, milk dribbled down Blossom's chin, and Lily's fingertips were slobbery. She couldn't stop worrying that the calf was not eating enough.

The camp was quiet around them, and she had an awareness of Coop standing guard—of the danger that Irene represented somewhere out in the woods. She felt a pang of pity for the woman who was so desperate for that jewel, so completely alone.

Lily looked up to see Paul splash cream from a tin pitcher into the bowl. Then Alex drizzled in molasses, dark and sticky.

"You try it! Stir slow so ya don't melt the ice." Alex handed Matt a spoon.

Matt took it with an amused expression on his face.

Their eyes met, and she didn't know what to do with the breathless feeling that rose inside her. She'd felt the same way moments ago when he'd asked whether she had eaten. That he knew and cared that her discomfort and nauseated feeling from earlier had gone. It felt warm and settling to know that he cared about her—about the baby. Was it just their adventure in the night that connected them together?

"Try it," Paul nodded to Matt, who lifted the spoon from the bowl and took a tentative taste. His brows lifted. "It's good."

She tied off Blossom with the tether, finished with the milk now.

"Ma made it better." Paul's eyes shadowed, and Alex put a hand to his brother's shoulder. Matt watched the show of brotherly affection, eyes hooded, a quiet yearning flickering across his face.

Lily frowned. Had he ever experienced a brother's love? The little bit that he'd told her about his growing-up years reminded her of what he hadn't had, and a memory sparked. She'd been nine; it had been Christmastime. She'd woken to a gift of soft, gray knitted mittens folded at her bed's foot. Stella and Maddie had watched her and shared her excitement, though they'd received only small peppermint sticks. She'd still believed Pa was a good father—

Now, looking back, she knew he had been in his cups even more deeply at Christmas, one of Mam's favorite times of year. Stella and Maddie must've scraped pennies for weeks to buy that yarn. The memory made Lily's current tension with Stella all the worse. They'd stayed close through a difficult childhood, only to grow apart now?

Alex's voice pierced her thoughts. "Can we give some to Mr. Coop?"

Paul seemed eager, too. It was broad daylight, and the woods were a bit off. Surely it was all right.

"Come right back," she said.

They dashed off. She stepped away from Blossom as Matt closed the distance between them. She was careful to keep her weight off her injured foot, still aching but not as terribly as earlier when she'd had to put her weight on it to climb that hill.

She realized Matt still held the spoon.

"I saved a bite for you."

Warmth bloomed in her cheeks as she took the spoon from him and ate the sweet, cold bite. His eyes seemed locked on her as he licked a drop of molasses from his thumb, and she couldn't help the way her breath stuck in her throat.

"Those boys are something," he said.

"You're good with them."

He seemed surprised by her compliment, his brows pulling together slightly.

She tucked a wind-loosened strand behind her ear. "Maddie's worried Irene might try for them next." Her eyes darted to where they were with Coop—safe.

Matt shifted. He kicked at a pebble near his boot, sending it skittering away. "You care about them, too." There was something raw and guarded in his tone.

Words spilled free. "I didn't mean to get so attached. I grew up in a wretched tenement in Dublin. Stella and Maddie shielded me from a lot of the difficult parts of our life there. I thought everyone had thin walls, little food, and the uncertainty of where the next meal would come from. I loved the other children—our neighbors. For a time, I dreamed of teaching." The long-forgotten dream stirred awake. It was easier to watch the boys than meet Matt's watchful gaze as they stood shoulder to shoulder.

"So you've always had a nurturing heart?" he asked.

"I never thought of it that way." Lily played with the edge of her shawl. His eyes flicked to her, then drifted to the wagon as if distracted. He rubbed the back of his neck.

"Do you miss your friends from Ireland?" His voice dipped, intimate against the camp's hum.

"I didn't have many. They were younger children on our floor, but only Megan was my age."

"Were you close?"

Lily's fingers twisted in her shawl. She turned slightly, her gaze catching on the dying fire. Only a few sparks drifting upward. "She lived next door. We grew up together —until I turned fifteen."

She hadn't thought about Megan in months. Remembering those days put a dull ache behind her breastbone. "Her father came into money—an inheritance. Enough to leave those awful tenements behind."

"She moved away?"

Lily nodded. Her fingers had clutched the shawl tighter without conscious thought. "I cried every night after she told me they were leaving. The day they went away, she promised to write, but I never got a letter. It was like she vanished from the world—like I wasn't good enough to be her friend anymore." The old hurt surged at the words.

He shifted, their elbows brushing. "That was her loss. I can't imagine someone not wanting to be your friend." There was a tone—something she couldn't read—in his words.

Face hot, she shrugged. A throb of pain went through her foot. Too much standing. "She was more outgoing than me—bright, almost wild. When we joined the other kids, she always saved me a spot in the game. She was so full of life."

Paul and Alex darted past, shouting that they were going to give some ice cream to Maddie. He met her gaze. "You deserved a better friend than her."

Lily cleared her throat. "After that, it was hard to trust anyone but my sisters."

A flash of understanding lit his eyes. She looked down, heart thrumming in her ears.

"You trusted Harry."

Hearing his name jolted her. Had she truly trusted Harry? The man she'd fancied herself in love with had wooed her and then seemingly abandoned her. When Harry'd come to her with a heartfelt apology and begged forgiveness, she'd been... relieved. Relieved that if her suspicions that she was carrying a baby were right, she wouldn't be alone.

But their time together, hers and Harry's, had been so short. Had she really had time to learn to trust him?

Grief and guilt pierced sharp as a blade. Had she thought of him today—on that brutal climb or amid the boys' laughter? The ache surged, making her throat raw.

"What about you?" she blurted. "Why did you leave the city?"

There was a prolonged beat of silence and then his expression shuttered. He stuffed his hands into his pockets and took a step back. "I better go—they'll need me on watch."

Surprised by his abrupt departure, she couldn't help

watching as he nodded to someone behind her and strode off past Stella, who approached with a frown. Why had Matt left so abruptly?

Stella's gaze tracked Matt, then fixed on Lily, sharp and stern. "Why are you spending time with another hired hand?"

The words held accusation, obliterating instantly the memory of those softer times with her sister back in Dublin. "I don't know what you mean," she snapped.

Stella's lips pinched. "You were leaning awful close—"

"I can't walk on my foot."

"What was he even doing here?"

"Checking on me."

Stella's smile showed a hint of triumph. "You're getting too close again—and after everything with Harry." Her disdain and the judgment from this morning, before Stella had realized that Lily was in peril, struck Lily's temper like a match on kindling.

"No," Lily bit out. "I'm not."

The bugle blared. Stella looked disappointed. But she left without another word.

Lily watched her go hitch the oxen, fury simmering in her chest.

Stella still saw her as a child—fragile and foolish. Why couldn't she see Lily as she was—a grown woman capable of taking care of herself?

Chapter Seven

TWILIGHT DRAPED the wagon camp in shadows, a chill settling over the frost-kissed ground as the faint tang of pine threaded through the air. Rob put away the pot he'd cooked his supper in.

He couldn't stop thinking about Alice's statement from days ago. *My brothers will never forgive you, and neither will I.* The words were a burr he couldn't shake. He'd never considered himself prideful. Grandfather often thought others beneath him, but Rob knew that everyone had value. But the idea of reconciling with Coop—reckless, hotheaded Coop, who'd punched him without provocation—made his teeth grind. Leo and Collin weren't any better, glaring across camp whenever they spotted him, making it clear they thought very little of him.

But Alice—she was worth losing a bit of pride, wasn't she? Perhaps if he had a chance to talk to Coop, they could call a truce.

Rob spotted him now, slipping between two wagons, glancing over his shoulder. Suspicion rose. What was Coop doing? Determination warred with the sour twist in his stomach as he followed from a distance. The company had grown quiet as dusk had fallen.

Coop paused behind a wagon, leaning to peek around as if he was watching—someone or something? Nothing moved in the woods nearby, but that's where Coop's focus seemed to be.

Rob cleared his throat. He stepped forward, his boots scuffing the frost-hardened earth. "I need a word."

A rustle snapped from the woods—a shadow bolted away.

"Wait!" Coop called out, his coat flapping open as he darted forward then jogged toward the treeline. Completely ignoring Rob. "Please, come back." His voice was low and urgent, but whatever—or whoever—Coop was seeking had vanished.

Coop stood staring into the shadowed woods. Everything was still and quiet. Coop's shoulders heaved, his fists clenching at his sides.

Rob had followed a few steps behind, and now Coop rounded on him, fury etching his face, closing the gap in three angry strides.

Coop's palms slammed into Rob's chest, the force jolting him. "Why'd you do that?"

Rob stumbled a step back, but Coop followed, eyes blazing.

When Coop took a swing, Rob ducked away. The

glancing blow found his shoulder. Pain flared, and he grunted, twisting aside. And then Coop was too close—his hands gripping Rob's shirt, yanking forward while Rob tried to push him off. Rob shoved at Coop's chest, straining against the grip. They grappled, boots scuffling.

"Get off!" Rob bit out. He jabbed an elbow upward but couldn't twist free.

"Your sneaking around scared her off!"

Her?

Rob had taken boxing lessons from a tutor, but Coop fought dirty, twisting Rob's skin and shirt cruelly beneath his fingers. Rob's temper flared, and his arm snapped up, fist connecting with Coop's jaw, the impact reverberating through his bones as Coop's head jerked back. Finally, he shoved the other man away.

"I wasn't sneaking," he snapped. He swiped a gloved hand across his mouth. "I just wanted to talk." He breathed hard, struggling to rein in his fraying temper.

Coop was breathing hard too, his chest rising and falling. He mumbled so that Rob barely caught the words, "I've been watching for days." Coop's gaze flicked toward the woods as if he couldn't help looking.

Alice. Rob thought her name, forced calm when he felt none. He took a slow breath, his hands unclenching as he exhaled. Her brother might be a hotheaded louse, but this wasn't about Coop. Rob had to think of Alice.

Rob lifted his hands to show that he meant no harm. "I came to talk about Alice." He kept his voice low, his words clipped with the leftover heat simmering in his chest.

Coop worked his jaw where Rob had hit him. "What about her?"

"Alice and I have a history." Relief swamped him. She'd always been the one who pushed for secrecy; he'd never understood. He'd wanted everyone—including her family—to know she belonged with Rob.

"Liar!" Coop's voice rasped with fury.

"We were friends." *And more.* But he wouldn't say that to her brother, not when Coop was so furious. "That's why I rode with her to fetch the soldiers—and Hollis."

Coop snorted. He spat into the snow, his lip curling as he leaned forward on his toes. "Should I organize a parade for you? Anybody would've done that—anybody with a conscience."

Rob knew the words were an insult to Grandfather. He had heard whispers in the powder mill, in ballrooms, and business meetings. His grandfather had a reputation for being hard-nosed, a stickler for the rules, a difficult business-man. He was a great success, even if others didn't agree with his methods.

Coop knew those words would hurt. Rob could read it in the spark in Coop's eyes.

Rob swallowed angry words that wanted to burst out. "I want our friendship back—mine and Alice's." He wanted more—and he would have it. Resolve hardened in his chest.

"Friendship? You think I'd let her near you after what your family did to ours?" Coop scoffed. "You're dreaming. Stay clear of her, or you'll regret it."

The words hit like a brick, shattering Rob's good intentions. "And if I don't?" His voice rose as he met Coop's glare.

Coop loomed closer, his eyes blazing.

"You don't get to control your sister's life." Rob thrust his hands out to block Coop's advance.

Coop lunged forward, a low grunt escaping as he swung his fist in an arc toward Rob's jaw. Rob ducked, grabbing Coop's arm, his fingers clamping tight around Coop's sleeve as he pulled Coop off balance. They grappled again in a near-silent tangle of shoving and twisting. Their breaths mingled in sharp puffs. Coop landed a blow to Rob's midsection. Air rushed from his lungs and he lost his breath. His vision blurred.

"Stop," a woman's voice gasped. The word halted both men mid-struggle.

Alice stood ten feet off, the lantern in her hand casting a gold glow across her face. Its light flickered as she raised it higher, her eyes were wide with shock. "What do you think you're doing?" Her glare softened when she glanced toward Coop. "Aren't you supposed to be on watch?"

Coop crossed his arms, his shoulders squared as he planted his feet, his intention clear—he was not leaving while Rob remained near his sister.

Alice glanced between them, frowning.

"I'd like to talk with you, Alice," Rob said, voice rough. He straightened, taking a moment to brush off his coat, straighten his shirt where Coop had grabbed onto him.

With a resigned look, she exhaled, her breath clouding in the chill air. "Leave my family alone."

Coop sent Rob a triumphant look before he and Alice walked off together, leaving Rob stewing. He'd meant to extend an olive branch. It wasn't his fault he'd interrupted Coop's sneaking around. He took off his hat and raked a hand through his hair.

Her words echoed in his ears. *Leave my family alone.* His hands clenched at his sides, his breath hitching as he turned away, his gaze going unfocused as her words sank deep, a bitter twist coiling in his gut.

She couldn't have made her choice more clear.

A chill nipped at Matt's exposed neck as he shifted in his saddle, the leather creaking beneath him. His horse snorted, and Matt imagined the breath puffing out white—he couldn't actually see it because it was dark on his middle of the night watch. His rifle rested in its scabbard, a cold weight against his thigh—a reminder of Irene out there somewhere.

The Fairfax wagon wasn't far away. Its white canvas caught the dying campfire's glow. He edged his horse closer. Tents clustered inside the circled wagons. Everyone was asleep except for the watch. Lucky was somewhere in the darkness out to his right, Gerry to his left around the circle, out of sight. He eyed the Fairfax wagon again. There were two tents near it. He figured Maddie and the children— Paul, Alex, and little Jenny—were tucked in one of them; Lily must be in the other. Matt's fingers tightened on the reins, leather biting into his palms. He couldn't shake his unease after he'd spent time with her and the boys earlier today.

What was it about her that drew him so? Was it only that she reminded him of Elsie? Elsie had been the one soft spot in his difficult growing-up years. Lily wasn't her match in personality—but they had the same color eyes. There'd been a hardness to Elsie, one that Matt was sure matched his own at that age—a toughness from having to fight for every scrap of food, any little bit of warmth.

Sometimes, when he caught the edge of Lily's smile, he saw a hint of Elsie—that had to be it.

Except he couldn't be Lily's friend. Amos's deadline was drawing closer. And Irene was out there, possibly standing in his way.

Amos had promised Matt a new salary once the ruby was in his hand. The money was the security Matt had always wanted—and he was planning to reward himself with a pocket watch. He'd be able to afford a better place to stay, maybe even buy some fancy duds. Those thoughts drove him to edge his horse closer to the wagons and glance around to see if the other watchmen were anywhere close. Everything was clear and quiet.

He swung down from the saddle, his boots softly crunching against the ground. He crept toward the Fairfax wagon—the fire was almost out; every shadow held a menacing bent as he remembered that Irene had had no qualms about shooting at him.

He strained his ears, dropped low, and then rolled to his back beneath the wagon. If it had been up to him, he would hide a jewel as valuable as the ruby in a compartment beneath. He let his eyes grow accustomed to the low firelight and studied the crossbeams, the side rails, and the floorboards. Nothing looked unusual—and there was no strongbox.

A damp chill from the earth seeped through his coat as he stared at the underside of the wagon. He took his gloves off, stuffed them in his pockets, then he ran his fingers along each plank, feeling for anything out of the ordinary—any kind of crack. He even covered the brake mechanism and every spoke on each one of the wheels.

A sudden voice—Paul's?

A single mumbled word.

Matt froze, heart slamming against his ribs. Was he caught?

No rustle followed—no one stirred. A soft snore. Perhaps the boy talked in his sleep?

Matt tipped his head back to see beneath the doubletree —still nothing.

Stella was clever—was it possible she was wearing the ruby around her neck? It would be risky, knowing Irene was after it. Frustration flared hot, driving him to crawl out from beneath the wagon. He rounded the tailgate, glanced around. Still no one stirred or awakened to notice his movements. Could he unlatch the tailgate without a clatter? Probably not. His fingers were cold as he worked to untie the canvas, the faint rustle of the fabric seeming far too loud in the stillness. He pushed the cover apart, revealing a jumble of crates, barrels, and sacks stacked high—everything a blur of shadow in the bare glow of a fire that was near embers.

There was no way to work through it before his absence would be noticed—he would need to unload every item, sift through the sacks of flour, the barrels of beans, look for any loose floorboard from the top. If Collin caught him, his ruse would be over.

His one chance—and he was going to fail.

Determination pierced him. Could he force Stella to give it to him?

A soft bleat pierced the quiet, intruding on Matt's racing thoughts. The calf was tethered near Lily's tent, and it awoke, its hoof scuffing the ground.

Matt's stomach plummeted. Before he could duck behind the wagon or return to his horse, a tent flap snapped open. Lily crawled out, her shawl clutched tightly around her shoulders, her hair in a long braid down her back. Fiery strands framed her face, and her beauty struck him like a blow, stealing his breath. Fumbling, he slipped a small item from his pocket into his palm.

Lily blinked sleepily, her steps edging toward him, still with a slight limp.

"Matt?" she whispered. "What are you doing here?"

He forced a grin, scrambled for an answer, feigned an easygoing attitude.

The calf bleated again.

"I brought this for you." He held out his hand. "I found it on the trail a fair piece ago. Thought it might be useful for your calf."

Lily's brows knit, her gaze flicking from him to the wagon. As she moved toward him, her shawl slipped slightly to reveal the curve of her nightdress-covered shoulder. Something tugged hard inside his stomach as she took the small item from his palm, curved her fingers around it for a moment before she looked at it.

A small metal bell.

He couldn't read the emotions crossing her expressive face.

The calf made another noise, this time tugging against its tether. Lily jumped, turning away with her head ducked as she slipped the bell into her pocket.

She took a bucket from inside the wagon, brushing past him momentarily, and pulled out a pouch of some sort. He heard the soft splash of liquid as she crossed to the calf. He followed a few steps behind, knowing she was aware of him by the way her head turned slightly.

"What are you really doing here?" She didn't look at him, even though her whisper was a challenge. "It's late. Everyone's asleep."

He thought of the ruby.

"I can't stop thinking about you." The words spilled free before he could rein them in. Foolish. Why had he said that?

He could see enough of Lily's face to see her mouth firmed into a hard line, a flicker of fear—or awareness—crossing her face. As she stood, wrapping her arms around herself, the calf butted her leg, forcing her to take a step to keep her balance.

"I'm not looking for a husband," she said, her voice steady. "Or a father for my baby."

Was that where her thoughts had gone? Her words would've stung if the moment of affection had been real. The canvas remained open behind him. If she thought he had courting on his mind, he'd let her think that. He pretended disappointment. "What about a friend, then? Nothing more."

"A friend," she repeated, her voice barely a whisper.

A friend might deserve to know where the ruby was. The words to ask were right on his lips.

"I mean it," he said instead. "You've been through enough. I just... wanted to make sure you were all right."

Her lips parted, a breath escaping. Her braid swayed as she turned to the calf. "You should go back to your watch."

But his feet were rooted to the ground.

Lily knelt beside the calf, in the darkness. She was aware of Matt watching her as her knees pressed into the cold earth, the damp seeping through her skirt as she adjusted her grip on the calf's makeshift feeder. The night chill was biting through her shawl. The dying campfire's embers cast a faint, flickering glow across the ground.

The silence surrounding them made their conversation seem more intimate. She tilted her head to avoid his steady gaze. Her hands trembled faintly.

What he'd said—*I just want to make sure you're all right*

—would've been just what she had wanted to hear if Harry had said them. Her throat tightened. She bit her lip, the sting of guilt prickling sharp as she thought of the man she'd planned to marry.

She was only responding to Matt's kindness because she didn't want to feel so alone—that had to be it. Things were still tilted with Stella, her sister barely speaking to her. Maddie was busy nursing others and caring for the kids. With her injured foot, Lily had ridden in the wagon all day alone, with thoughts of the baby and the uncertain future plaguing her.

She fiddled with the contraption she'd rigged up earlier, poured milk into the makeshift pouch, her fingers fumbling with the bladder's slick surface as milk sloshed faintly inside it. Then she offered the slight protrusion to the calf. She steadied it with both hands as the calf nudged against her. She felt the weight of Matt's gaze, aware that she hadn't answered his question of friendship. Heat rose in her cheeks despite the cold.

Blossom lapped greedily, her rhythmic sucking sharp against the quiet. When the calf nudged the makeshift udder, Lily steadied it with a shaky hand.

Matt squatted beside her. "What's that?"

She glanced sidelong at him. Embarrassment prickled sharp as she kept an eye on the contraption, making sure Blossom wasn't destroying it with her enthusiasm.

"It's a bladder," she mumbled, her voice small against the night's expanse. "From a buffalo we took earlier on the trail." She shifted her feet as Blossom tugged harder. Her injured foot throbbed slightly. "I cut a finger off an old glove and sewed it on. A man-made udder for her to drink from."

She braced for his scorn, remembering Stella's wrinkled nose when she'd glimpsed Lily working on her project earlier.

"That's clever, Lily."

His soft praise bloomed warmth in her chest, a flicker of pride, an encouragement she hadn't known she needed. It was working, wasn't it? Blossom was guzzling the milk—only she was at the dregs of her last bucket. "I'll need to source more milk if she keeps eating like this." She tilted the bladder as the last drops dribbled out. "It's a shame about her mama."

Lily hadn't been able to stop thinking about the cow's tragic end. Could she have been saved if Lily had made a different choice? Hadn't waded in after old Ezra? The calf would be better off with a mother to feed her.

A beat of silence. He shifted beside her, his coat rustling quietly. "You didn't answer me before—but maybe that's answer enough."

She thought of the bell in her pocket, his thoughtfulness. All day she'd tried to ignore the way her heart beat faster when she saw him from across camp. Yet guilt swamped her. Harry had only been dead two weeks, and now she was drawn to Matt. Was it wrong?

She stilled as he rose slowly, adjusted his hat, his breath visible in the chill air.

"I... know about losing someone you love. I don't—I only remember bits of my parents now. My ma hugging me to her, a laugh that I think was my pa's. Sometimes a scent makes me feel like I can almost remember..." He shook his head, seemed to come to himself. He met her gaze again, his eyes softening as he shoved his hands into his coat pockets. "The offer stands—if you need help, or someone to talk to, I'd like to be your friend. At least until we get to the end of this trail and I go back east."

She straightened suddenly, her injured foot twinging as she steadied herself. Some invisible tension pulled in the air between them. Her breath hitched. She brushed her skirt, her fingers trembling as she glanced at him.

His horse huffed from outside the circle of light. The sound cut through the quiet, and he tilted his head toward it. "I've got to get back to the watch." He strode into the dark but glanced over his shoulder, his hand lifting to tip his hat.

He couldn't know how his words, a reminder of the journey's end, had thrown her into turmoil. They still had weeks of travel left, but she hadn't known he didn't intend to stay in Oregon. If she let their friendship develop, perhaps he would tell her that he would write—her hand slipped back into her pocket, her fingers curling tight around the bell as her chest ached. He might promise they would always be friends from a distance.

But Megan hadn't written Lily, even though she had only lived a handful of miles away.

She couldn't imagine letters being exchanged across the vast wilderness. Surely it was a gamble whether a letter would reach its recipient at all. Perhaps it would take months to hear from him once he went back East.

No, any friendship between them would be short-term. It would have an end date. And she wasn't sure she could face another loss. Her breath shuddered as a hint of panic fluttered beneath her ribs.

She stared into the darkness, her eyes tracing the shadowed pines, the pull of panic rising completely as she thought of the danger still ahead—the mountain crossings, more rivers to ford, and Irene, who was still somewhere out there.

Inside her pocket, her fingers curled tighter around the bell. She wanted to call after Matt, ask him to come back, to stay with her and just talk. Her lips parted, a faint sound escaping as she took a step forward, but then she choked back the words.

Building a friendship wouldn't be fair to either of them, not when it couldn't last.

Chapter Eight

TWO DAYS HAD PASSED with no sign of Irene or any other danger. Lily's ankle was much improved, and Maddie had asked her to drive Doc's wagon today so that Maddie and Jason could work on a young boy who had suffered a fall and a badly broken arm. Paul and Alex had been tasked with herding Blossom up the mountain and had fallen back several wagons as they chatted with Felicity and young Ben. Or at least that's where they'd been last time Lily had checked.

Maddie had also asked Lily to watch over Jenny. Lily was thankful that the young girl had become sleepy, and she laid her in the front part of Maddie's wagon that had been partitioned off with crates and lined with a quilt. Had Maddie seemed cagey when she'd told Lily not to look in the back of the wagon, just to tend Jenny in the front?

Now the line of wagons crept up a narrow trail at what seemed like the very top of this mountain, single file around a hairpin turn. Lily walked beside the oxen, on the inside, closest to the mountain itself, and near enough to the wagon to be able to hear if Jenny woke. A light rain had begun to fall an hour ago. Its soft patter drummed gently on Lily's shawl and the wagon's canvas, a muted rhythm against the stillness.

Lily had to work to keep her eyes from skittering to the other side of the wagon, where the cliff dropped in a dizzying plunge, meeting a misty valley far below. An occasional pine pierced the fog like a ghostly sentinel, its branches clawing through the haze. Even the oxen seemed to understand the danger of this crossing, because the ornery lead one wasn't attempting to veer from the path.

There'd been a fine tension in camp since the news of Irene following Stella and Maddie and Lily had spread through the company. Some folks had chosen to keep their distance, while others, like Collin's family, had drawn close to help with keeping watch, especially over the vulnerable children.

Stella hadn't spoken to Lily in the past two days. And she'd only seen Matt from a distance.

Leo and Collin seemed to be running the hired hands ragged, asking for extra hours on watch and having them ride on horseback alongside the wagons instead of herding the cattle.

Lily felt lonelier than ever.

After deciding it was better to keep her distance from Matt, she spent some time with Alex and Paul in the evenings after the wagons had circled up, but after they were sent to bed, there was no one for her to talk to—not with Maddie busy with the folks who needed nursing, and Stella keeping her distance.

Was this what it would be like when they reached Oregon? Lily would have to figure out a way to have a house built. Or perhaps she could find a room to rent. But what would she do to raise money to feed herself and the baby when it came along?

Blossom was the one bright thing in Lily's days. The calf seemed to know that Lily was the one providing its food, so she pranced around and butted at Lily's thighs when it was time for feeding. She'd taken to following Lily everywhere she went.

A whistle sounded from somewhere behind. Lily craned her neck to see where it had come from. She knew that August was not able to scout anymore, but Hollis had called two of the other men to ride out in front, to scout their path and watch for danger.

Suddenly, a sharp crack split the air. Doc's wagon lurched. The wheels rolled forward. The wagon tipped at a precarious angle. Lily ducked to look beneath, to see if a wagon wheel had busted, only to find that the axle had snapped in two.

The oxen continued pulling in their traces, but the wagon couldn't move correctly. As she peered beneath the conveyance, the narrow path crumbled beneath the broken front wheel. Dust and pebbles skittered off the edge of the cliff.

Inside the wagon, crates and barrels thudded, shifting

around. With the wagon tipped toward the front right corner, this nearest corner was too high for her to see inside. Had Jenny been injured?

"Help! Someone, please!" Her cry echoed off the rock wall.

What if the little girl was crushed by a heavy crate?

Lily commanded the oxen to halt, but with the wagon tilted and the doubletree in an awkward position, the animals appeared panicked and were still attempting to pull. Even so, she scrambled to try and climb up into the wagon seat. Maybe she could grab Jenny from there.

But her feet slipped with the wagon tilted away from her. Jenny shrieked and cried from inside.

What should she do?

She quickly rounded the back of the wagon, even as an indistinct shout rang out from someone in the wagon behind. There was nowhere for the wagons following hers to go. The trail was too narrow, the cliffside too close for them to pass. Her legs trembled as she lunged to the side-board of the wagon, aware of the cliff's edge only inches behind her feet. Where the front wheel tilted at an awkward angle, the ground beneath continued to crumble away.

"Lily, get back!" Matt's voice, coming from somewhere nearby. Hoofbeats echoed, but she didn't dare turn her head and risk looking down into the abyss below.

"Can you steady the oxen?" she called over her shoulder in a tremulous voice. She edged her way toward the front of the wagon, bracing herself against Jenny's wails from inside.

If she hurried too fast, she might slip and fall down the cliffside.

"Lily, don't!" That was Matt's voice. She didn't turn her head, but he sounded like he might be right behind the wagon.

"I can't!" She took another careful step, clinging to the sideboard.

"Come back from there!"

In her peripheral vision, she caught sight of the immense drop off below. When she spoke, fear had stolen all her breath and the words were barely audible. "Jenny's inside."

"Just come back and I'll get her."

She couldn't turn back now. She was almost there. She reached the front corner. The ground was so soft that her boots threatened to sink into it. She gritted her teeth against the fear clawing at her throat.

"Here, Jenny. I'm right here." She fumbled with the canvas even as she heard more stones and soil skitter and fall away. Was Matt coming around the corner of the wagon?

There was nowhere safe for her to put her weight on this edge. Jenny's wail grew louder. "Ma—Ma—Ma."

Lily didn't know whether she was calling for her mother or Maddie or just shrieking out of fear.

Finally, Lily got the canvas pulled back enough to see Jenny wedged against the corner of the wagon. The crates had shifted, and though she wasn't being smothered, a barrel wobbled atop what was now a jumble of supplies, ready to fall in the child's direction any moment.

Aware of Matt's slow sideways approach, Lily reached

inside the wagon with both arms, wedging her elbows to try and hold herself against the conveyance. She put her hands beneath Jenny's arms and gave a careful tug, aware that if one of the girl's legs was wedged in the wagon, she might injure her.

Someone shouted from the opposite side of the wagon, out of sight, and the oxen began to pull harder. The wagon shuddered, unable to move correctly on its broken axle. Lily began to lift Jenny out of the wagon, aware of someone edging their way around from the direction Lily herself had come. Jenny was free of the canvas. Lily pulled the girl tightly to her shoulder, gripping the wagon sideboard with her other hand.

"Lily!" Matt's voice rose in warning again. She turned her head slightly and glimpsed his face, stark with the same terror she was feeling. "We've got to get clear—"

Before he finished the sentence, the wagon shuddered, pulling forward. The ground beneath Lily's feet gave way in a muddy cascade, a treacherous roar of earth and stone. Lily lost her grip on the wagon. She cried out as she began to fall.

Matt felt the wagon shake from where his left hand clung to the sideboard, saw it as if in slow motion as the ground vanished beneath Lily, leaving only a void that fell to the valley below. He lunged forward as Lily screamed, going to his knees on the narrow patch of ground beside the wagon. His fingers clamped tight on Lily's rain-slicked arm. Desperation surged hot in his veins as the muddy ground beneath her sent her sliding away.

The force of taking her weight yanked him forward. More shale crumbled beneath his weight. He kept hold of her arm as they tumbled together, his shoulder banging hard against the rock wall. They crashed onto a small, rocky ledge, maybe eight or ten feet beneath the wagon resting precariously on the narrow trail.

Mist swirled thick around them, the valley still yawning below. Relief crashed through his chest as he pulled Lily into him, as they huddled beside the rock wall with the little girl between them. His heart slammed hard against his sternum, a frantic drumbeat, as rain dripped steadily from his hat brim down the back of his neck, chilling his skin.

Her breath hitched—not a sob. Her eyes were wide with terror and filling quickly with tears. He wrapped one arm around her waist, and her trembling body pressed even closer. He glimpsed a protruding tree root above him and raised his arm to wrap his hand around it for extra security. The root was rough and slick under his fingers, but it offered an anchor to the ledge.

The little girl had stopped shrieking. Now, her tear-filled brown eyes stared up at Matt's face.

"They went over!" a shout rang out from the rocky trail above them. Matt craned his neck back. Lily did, too.

There were more shouts from above. And then, as Matt squinted, he glimpsed Rusty's silhouette at the cliff's edge. The wagon—not the Fairfax's, maybe Doc's—was still up there, out of commission, probably because of a broken axle, if his guess was correct.

"There they are!" Rusty had seen them. Another beat of relief flooded through Matt.

He gently squeezed Lily's waist. "They're gonna figure out a way to get us up."

She glanced to the side, down into the faraway valley, and shivered, turning to press her face into his shoulder.

"It's all right," he said quietly. "We're safe for now."

"What if the ground gives away?"

"Can't think like that," he said quickly. "There's probably a big boulder cut into the mountainside right beneath our feet. It won't take long before they send a rope down."

"Jenny can't climb a rope. I don't think I can either."

She was running through all the worst-case scenarios, thinking of every disaster that might happen. If she let herself get well and truly panicked, she might be too scared to get up that rope when it came down.

"What if the wagon falls on top of us—" She had raised her face from his shoulder and seemed to be staring straight ahead, eyes unfocused.

He nudged her cheek with his nose.

The movement must've startled her; she tipped her head up slightly, her eyes widening as her searching gaze found his face. For a moment, he couldn't look away from her beauty —the rain-soaked hair clinging to her temples, the way her eyelashes clumped together. A wave of warmth crashed over him, stole his breath, and he did the only thing he could think of in that moment. He bent his head and brushed his lips over hers.

He meant only to stop her panicked words, break her loose from the terror holding her in its grip, but the moment his chilled lips brushed hers, she let out what might've been the tiniest huff of air—surprise?—and he couldn't help himself. He slanted his lips over hers when she responded sweetly. The misty rain mingled with the heat of her mouth, her breath a trembling sigh against his, a fleeting spark in the cold.

More shouts from above broke the moment. He leaned back, out of breath. She stared at him with wide eyes, lips parted in shock. He wanted to pull her even closer, though he was conscious of the girl between them, snuggled to Lily's shoulder.

"Here comes the rope!" Rusty called out.

Lily glanced away, giving him her profile. She was silent now, and he could only hope that his attempt to shock her out of her building panic had worked. This wasn't the moment to talk about what had just transpired between them.

"Is the little one all right?"

Lily shook her head slightly, as if coming out of a daze, and glanced down into Jenny's face. The girl had stuffed her thumb in her mouth and seemed to be chewing on it worriedly.

"I think so."

The rope knocked dust and tiny rocks atop their heads.

Matt leaned his head close to Lily so the rim of his hat shielded both her and Jenny.

And then the rope was there.

When Matt glanced up again, Collin had joined Rusty at the cliff's edge.

They couldn't stay down here; they needed to get up that hillside. He gripped the rope, its fibers slick and cold. "I'm going to tie this around you. They'll pull you up." He wrapped it carefully beneath Lily's arms and tied it off in front of her, showing her how to wrap it once around her wrist for extra hold. "Can you get up with the little one?"

She turned terrified eyes on him. Her lips were pinched in a white line, but she nodded, eyes wide.

"Bring her up!" he called. Rusty and Collin both carefully pulled hand over hand, and Lily and Jenny were drawn up. She used her feet to keep them from banging into the cliff face.

As she moved over his head and then up and over the ledge, Matt was alone, gripping the root as rain dripped on his shoulders and his hat. He felt like he'd been thrown from a horse. The intensity of that kiss—the way she'd yielded to the press of his lips for that one fleeting moment—left him wanting more.

Her words from the campfire days ago echoed sharply in his mind. *I'm not looking for a husband.* His chest tightened.

Even if she were looking for a husband, Matt wasn't the kind of man she'd be looking for. He'd grown to know Collin, knew the man had a strong sense of morals. Doc, Maddie's husband, was upright and straight as an arrow. Lily would want someone like that—not someone who twisted the truth for a living, made a way for his boss to get around the law.

Matt wasn't worthy of her.

The rope lowered again, and Matt reached for it, rain streaming down the sleeve of his coat as he wrapped the rope around one wrist. He gripped it with his other hand, not waiting to tie it around himself. He gave Rusty a nod. The rope creaked as Rusty hauled him up. In only a few minutes, he emerged over the edge and collapsed onto the wet ground, breath ragged.

The wagon had been moved a few feet farther up the trail. It listed to the side even worse than before. He didn't know whether or not they would be able to move it again.

There was chaos everywhere. Maddie clutched Jenny, leaning over Lily, voice soft but urgent.

Lily sat with her back against the rock wall, as far from the cliff's edge as she could manage. She had a blanket wrapped around her and refused to meet his gaze.

He stepped over to her, swallowing back the urge to ask whether she was angry with him, whether she might forgive him for that kiss.

She glanced up, eyes wary. He knelt beside her, voice hushed. "What happened down there... It was a mistake. I shouldn't have done it."

He didn't know whether he really meant the words, but his hands fisted beside him.

Lily stared at him, silent. He longed for her to say something. Argue that he was wrong. Tell him she forgave him.

But she only remained drawn and silent, eyes shadowed.

When there was nothing left to say, he nodded to her and left her side as Maddie appeared, asking about cuts or scrapes.

Leo had joined Collin, and they were bent over, looking at the broken axle. More men had gathered from the wagons behind which were trapped on this hillside, unable to move forward because of the inoperable wagon.

Rusty came to stand next to Matt. Collin sent a wary look over his shoulder.

Leo spoke to his brother in a low voice, pointing at something that Matt couldn't see. "This wasn't an accident. Someone sabotaged this wagon."

Chapter Nine

ROB'S STOMACH gurgled with hunger. He crouched beside the lead ox, running a hand along its flank to steady it as twilight deepened around them. It was nearly dark, and he was considering taking his rifle and slipping into the woods nearby to shoot himself a squirrel or a rabbit.

Traversing the steep mountain pass was more treacherous than any terrain the company had encountered thus far. It somehow made his hunger sharper.

And it wasn't as if he could take the oxen from their traces and settle them for the night. Not while trapped on this mountainside. Something had happened to one of the wagons ahead. The path was too narrow for any other wagons to pass. They were as good as trapped here until the broken-down wagon could be moved.

Caleb Carter and his wife and kids were two wagons back from Rob. He could hear occasional snatches of the children's voices drifting on the chilly air.

Movement from ahead caught Rob's attention. Were they rolling out?

No. Leo picked his way carefully down the mountainside, boots crunching on loose gravel, and stopped to talk to the man and woman one wagon ahead of Rob. What was he saying? Rob couldn't hear anything other than the rumble of the man's voice. But he looked grim.

Rob lifted the ox's front hoof, balancing it on his knee as he scraped at a wedged pebble with a hoof pick, his fingers stiff from the cold. After a few moments, Leo began moving in Rob's direction. He glanced up once, and there was no mistaking the disdain in his expression. Rob bristled. Whatever message Leo was delivering seemed important enough to be delivered to every wagon personally—but would Leo skip over Rob?

He didn't. He stopped close enough for talking and rocked back on his heels.

"The axle on one of the wagons is busted. The wagon's good and stuck until we can repair it enough to get it off the cliffside."

That explained why the other wagons hadn't moved in so long.

"Do you need more manpower? I've got an ax," Rob offered, setting the hoof down gently and brushing dirt from his hands.

Leo shifted his stance. "Collin and a few others are working on it."

Leo glanced to his left, past Rob's oxen to the sweeping

vista of the valley below. A muscle jumped in his cheek. What wasn't he saying?

"We worked side by side at the mill," Rob reminded him, reaching for the ox's other hoof, checking for signs of thrush in the dim light. "If you need help—"

"We might've worked together, but no one in that powder mill mistook themselves as being your equal." Leo's words were cold.

If Rob ever had a chance of making him understand his feelings for Alice, this was his opening. "We were friends."

"We were never friends." Leo's eyes glittered. "Eddie Bell was my friend. When his little girl was sick with croup, I covered his shift for him, worked a double. Jimmy Patterson was my friend. When I got a bad cut on my hand, he patched me up on our meal break so I could finish my shift in the afternoon."

"If I had known, I would have finished your shift for you," Rob argued, his grip tightening on the hoof pick as he pried at another small stone.

"I needed that shift," Leo said. "To put food on the table for my sister."

The mention of Alice brought Rob up short. He lowered the ox's hoof, the beast snorting softly as he stood, wiping sweat from his brow despite the evening chill.

He had to remember what his true goal was: win over her brothers. Win her back.

"I worked just as hard as everyone on our shift," he said stiffly.

Leo was shaking his head, mouth a hard line. "Maybe so. But every worker on the line knew who you were. Knew that if they told the bawdy jokes they normally would have, there was a chance you'd report them to your granddad. Knew that if you were unhappy with their work, their job was at risk."

Rob turned to the ox's flank as Leo's words stung like a lash. He didn't want the other man to see his reaction.

He had grown up in his grandfather's household after his parents had passed away in a carriage accident when he was young. As a child, he'd been told to earn excellent marks in his lessons, delivered by a series of tutors. That when he grew up to run the powder mill, he'd need the knowledge they imparted.

When he'd been eighteen, his grandfather had sent him to work at the mill. He said Rob needed to gain experience, know the mill inside and out, starting on the line where the lowliest workers were placed.

He'd toiled at physical labor that was more difficult than anything he'd done in his entire life.

And believed that the men he was working with had become friends.

To hear Leo say otherwise now rattled him. Angered him. He'd worked just as hard as everyone else.

"I pulled my own weight working on the line with you," he said, his voice low as he leaned against the ox, the beast's warmth grounding him. "Worked just as long and as hard as you and Collin and Coop and the others."

Leo's eyes were like chips of ice. "You might've worked with us, but you were never one of us. Not really."

Rob's jaw clenched, and he busied himself checking the ox's harness, tugging at a strap to mask his frustration. He opened his mouth to argue further, but Leo was shaking his head. "I didn't come over here to argue with you." Leo sighed. "Hollis took the other half of the wagons, those that had already made it over this pass, and kept moving. The rest of us will circle up in a little valley on the other side of the pass, as soon as we can get that wagon moved." His nostrils flared, like what he meant to say next tasted bad.

"Seems like someone might be chasing us. Might've sabotaged that wagon. We need every able-bodied man to go on watch tonight once we get circled up."

There were shouts from somewhere ahead. Sounded like jubilation—maybe the men had been able to move the stuck wagon? Leo looked over his shoulder and then back at Rob, wearing an expectant expression.

"I didn't hear a question," Rob muttered, looping the hoof pick onto his belt and crossing his arms. "Or was that an order?"

Leo's brows bunched together at the challenge in Rob's voice. "We've got a lot of vulnerable women and children riding along with us. You'd let them suffer or be killed because we can't get along?"

"Of course not." Rob's answer came immediately. He reminded himself to think about Alice. A difficult relationship with her brothers wouldn't be something she would forgive.

Leo started to walk past Rob, presumably to share the instructions with the rest of the pioneers. Rob stopped him with an outstretched hand. He stepped away from the ox, his boots sinking slightly into the rocky earth. Met Leo's narrow gaze. "So we were never friends, you and I?"

Rob could remember many times when they had shared their lunches. Hours spent joking around together or discussing possible improvements to Grandfather's process. Would Leo completely ignore that time spent together?

Leo's words were cool and final. "If there was any friendship between us, it would've died when your grandfather let Coop take the blame for that explosion—and you didn't do a thing to stop it."

Matt rode into camp well after nightfall, after tailing the last of the cattle over that ridge and into the little valley beyond. It had taken hours to repair the axle on Maddie and Jason's wagon, and the half of the wagon train company stuck on the mountainside had moved so slowly through the pass that they couldn't catch up with the rest of the company. They'd camped in the next flat spot big enough to circle the wagons, the pioneers tense and terrified of what danger might be lurking somewhere in the wilderness, hunting them.

Matt was exhausted after a long day in the saddle and finally getting the cattle over the trail. He took care of his horse and ground-tied the animal with the other cowboys' horses, then took his hat off, running one hand through his hair as he headed toward the cowboys' campfire, this time right at the edge of the circled wagons. Leo and Collin seemed to be taking no chances.

His grumbling stomach reminded him that he had not eaten since breakfast that day, and his bed was calling him, though he knew he'd be wanted for a watch later in the night.

It hit him as he had been driving the cattle up that hill—he hadn't thought about the ruby once today. But he couldn't stop thinking about Lily, her pale face stark against the cliff's edge, the way she could've tumbled down that mountainside if he hadn't been there to catch her.

That kiss.

Now the ruby caught his thought, and it lodged in his throat as he realized Collin was awake and standing near the cowboys' campfire. Two men were tucked in their bedrolls, already snoring. Rusty and Gerry, likely.

What if he asked Collin for the ruby? Told him his true purpose. Told him that he could make the danger disappear by riding out with it. If Irene knew that Matt had the jewel, she would follow him and leave the wagon train alone.

Collin nodded as Matt neared, keeping his voice low. "Sleep for a few hours and then go on last watch."

Matt nodded. The words right there on the tip of his tongue. Instead, "Wagon all fixed up?"

Collin frowned. "We salvaged it, but I'm not sure the fix will last. If the axle fails, we'll load what we can into Stella's wagon and leave the rest." He ran a hand down his face. "If the wagon would've fallen on one of the kids, it would've crushed them."

It was God's providence that Matt had been close enough to jump off his horse and help rescue Lily and Jenny —at least that's what Rusty had said after he'd helped pull them up over the edge of that cliff. Matt wasn't sure he believed in God's providence, but Rusty was right. If he hadn't been there, Lily and Jenny might've fallen to their deaths.

"Do you think that woman sneaked into camp and filed through the axle?"

Collin shook his head. "I've been chewing on it all night."

"Lily said she wasn't in her right mind," Matt reminded him. "She was a terrible shot. Seemed weak. Probably starving if she hasn't been able to catch game or have any real food."

Collin looked grim. "I know. It makes me think there's someone else out there. Hollis fought off a lone man out in the woods weeks ago."

A man? Matt wanted to ask about this new information. Had his guess about Amos's henchman been correct?

"You should've seen the two men that tried to kidnap Maddie thinking to get the ruby. They were rough. Mercenaries," Collin said. "If there's someone else out there, someone like that..." He shook his head.

Matt knew what kind of men Amos employed when he needed to get things done.

If someone like an enforcer was out in the wild—not Irene—it could mean the company was in far more danger than Matt had thought. More reason to get the ruby and leave. Except Matt was torn. Desperately torn.

"I'll let you get some rest." Collin walked away, the weight of his exhaustion and worry clear in the slump of his shoulders.

Someone moved between the wagons.

The flickering firelight illuminated fiery hair, instantly recognizable as Lily's glow against the dark. She started toward him. He abandoned all thoughts of his bed to go to her.

"Better to stay close to camp," he said.

Her face was a pale smudge in the darkness. "I know. I saw you ride up."

"How's little Jenny?"

He caught the minute movement as her brows drew together. "She seems to be fine, though Maddie hasn't let go of her all evening." Her gaze flashed to him and then away.

"And you?" he pressed. "How are you?"

No answer came. Instead, she thrust something out toward him, and he realized she was holding a steaming plate of food. "I thought you'd be hungry."

Her words and the unexpected kindness stirred a warmth he hadn't expected.

"You didn't need to," he murmured. But he took the plate anyway, their fingers brushing. The heat from the tin seeped into his palm, even through his glove. "Been a long time since somebody has thought about feeding me."

Lily's head tilted as she studied him. "Has no one ever taken care of you before?"

Long-ago memories flickered, intangible, not something he could catch if he thought too hard about them.

"Not in a very long time," he said, stabbing at the beans, the fork scraping tin. "I did have some friends when I was a teenager. The streets—where I grew up—" He almost told her he was from New York City, something he hadn't admitted to yet. Would she connect him with the Byrnes brothers if he let that information slip? "I took factory work when I could, sweeping floors, hauling crates, working the machinery. There were four of us who watched out for each other."

Although it wasn't the same as the family ties he saw between Lily and her sisters. Even when he knew that Lily wasn't getting along with Stella, he had seen Stella hovering behind a wagon, watching Lily after they'd come up from nearly falling off that cliff. It was obvious that Stella loved her sister, even if they weren't getting along.

"It's different than your family. The way Maddie watches out for you. The way you'd do anything for your sisters."

A shadow flickered through her eyes, and she lowered her gaze, her nose wrinkling.

"One of my friends was a girl named Elsie. I told myself I fancied her."

After the kiss he'd shared with Lily today, he knew whatever he had felt for Elsie back then was a shadow of his feelings for Lily now. It couldn't have been real with Elsie. It hadn't lasted.

"One night she told me she was carrying a child—some

other fellow's kid. I was fifteen, dumb as a post, but I asked her to marry me, promised to take care of her." He swallowed hard, unable to eat another bite from the plate. "I thought getting married would fix things, thought I could be the man she needed."

He couldn't read Lily's expression, the slight draw of her brows. "She turned me down flat. After that, I moved on. She saw what I didn't know back then. I wasn't good for her."

He'd been alone on the streets for too long, fighting to survive. It had made him selfish. He would've protected himself before he protected Elsie. Somehow she'd known that.

"I see an honorable man," she said, the words barely audible. Her eyes flickered to him and then away, a shy dip of her chin.

Surprise hit him harder than what Collin had revealed only minutes ago.

And she wasn't finished. "You risked your life to save me and Jenny. Perhaps your Elsie would've regretted saying no if she saw who you are today."

Lily had it all wrong, and he almost opened his mouth to tell her so. She didn't know him—not really. Didn't know the real reason he'd come here, the reason he'd offered friendship in the first place.

But her admiration made him feel ten feet tall, like he could be the man she thought he was, if given a chance. He wanted to reach for her. So badly that he had to clench his hands into fists to keep from giving in to the urge. She remained half-turned away from him, head tipped toward the ground.

Looking down at her like this, remembering what they'd been through earlier, what he truly wanted, he suddenly didn't care whether he got the ruby or not. He wouldn't take it back to Amos now, even if Lily handed it to him herself.

Lily was a woman worth protecting. Maybe he would never be the man she thought he was, but he felt a visceral urge to protect her, to protect the people she loved.

* * *

A deep internal shiver shook Lily under Matt's intense gaze.

"Did you love her?" The whispered words tumbled from her lips, though she hadn't meant to say them aloud. Something inside her demanded to know.

When an answer didn't come, she raised her gaze to his face. He was staring at her in a way that was somehow affectionate and sorrowful and *hungry* all at the same time—

Before she could even blink, the expression vanished.

"No," he said quietly. "Maybe I could've, if things had ended up differently."

He didn't love his Elsie. Why did that knowledge cause some invisible band around Lily's chest to loosen?

She had prepared a speech and supper for him, ready to demand he explain that kiss, tell him that she still loved Harry—

But she couldn't force the words out, not with this invisible tension stretching between them, taut as a bowstring. Ready to snap.

A part of her wanted him to reach for her.

That wasn't fair either.

Everything was muddled now as she stood beside him, huddled in her shawl. Matt's clear surprise when she had brought the food touched something inside her. What had his life been like up to this point that he was surprised by basic kindness?

It wasn't only the compassion that stirred inside her and muddled things. It wasn't even the heat of his kiss, something she hadn't been able to stop thinking about all day.

It was realizing she could barely remember the feel of Harry's arms embracing her. That they had barely known each other. She knew more about Matt than she had about the man she had planned to marry, the man whose child she carried.

A rush of uncertainty smothered her and she felt the sob rising in her throat. She couldn't stand here any longer. Not without revealing something she couldn't even countenance to herself.

"I'll leave you to finish," she said quickly, aware that most of the company slept behind them. Heart pounding, she turned before he had a chance to argue or to reach for her or anything else.

His "Good night, Lily," was a whisper in the darkness.

She slipped back into the circle of wagons, aware that he was watching her. She moved out of his line of sight, stood leaning into the wood and canvas of Stella's wagon as she tried to steady her breath. What was she doing?

She should check on Blossom. But that only took a moment. The calf slept tethered to the wagon wheel.

Still unsettled, Lily couldn't keep herself from tiptoeing over to the tent Maddie shared with the children. She quietly pulled back the flap.

It took a moment for her eyes to adjust, to realize that the lumpy shadows were Alex and Paul, lying back to back. Maddie slept wrapped around Jenny as if afraid to let her go, even in sleep.

A bolt of fierce jealousy hit Lily, boiling from her midsection into her limbs. Sudden tears pressed behind her eyes. Maddie was so *blessed* to have those children in her life. Lily had experienced doubts when Maddie had first taken them on. But the boys were fiercely loyal to each other and to their little sister. And Jenny. She'd grieved for her lost mother in her own way, but she was a sweetheart. Maddie had bonded with them immediately. When she'd married Jason, the five of them had become a family.

Family. Something that Lily longed for more than anything.

She squeezed her eyes closed against the tears that wanted to fall. But closing her eyes was like being back on that cliffside in Matt's arms. She'd been trapped in a spiral of panic. Standing only inches from a precipice that meant certain death.

Matt's voice had broken through the haze of fear for only a moment, and then she'd been trapped again.

It was when he'd bent his head and kissed her that the maelstrom inside her had gone still and quiet. Her entire focus had shifted to the touch of his lips against hers. For long moments, she'd forgotten the peril completely.

Even when the kiss had ended, when there'd been men and busyness above them on the cliff, she'd found herself leaning into the strength of his arm around her. Breathless and wishing that it could be real. That the baby she was holding was her own child, safely delivered into the world. And in her fanciful imagining, she'd put Matt as her partner. Her husband.

Each time he'd protected her, her feelings for him had grown. From acquaintanceship to friendship to…

She couldn't think it.

Maddie stirred, her voice a sleepy murmur in the dark. "You all right, Lily?"

"Just needed to check on Jenny one more time."

Maddie moved slightly to reveal the toddler snug against her torso. Jason was probably on watch with the other men.

"She's safe," Maddie said sleepily. "We all are."

Lily nodded and whispered good night then tucked the tent flap closed. She slipped into her own tent, wrapped herself in her bedroll, and let one arm curve over her still-flat stomach.

Guilt and confusion birthed hot tears behind her eyelids. She closed her eyes, a silent storm in the dark.

She liked Matt. She could admit it to herself in the darkness of her tent. How could she be so fickle? Only weeks ago she had been sure Harry had captured her heart.

It was too fast.

Was Stella right? Had Lily let Matt get too close, gotten too attached? Shame seared her cheeks with heat. Matt had told her in no uncertain terms that he wasn't staying in Oregon once they arrived. Which meant that whatever feelings Lily was battling with right now, they wouldn't matter in a few months' time.

She needed to put her walls up, keep her heart guarded, keep her distance from him.

On the heels of that thought was the memory of Matt's vulnerability as he had admitted to the girl he once cared for. Her mind went to his fierceness, the wild determination she'd seen in his expression as he had grabbed ahold of her and the cliff had fallen away beneath them. He was protective. He encouraged her when she had been uncertain about taking care of Blossom.

Stella's warning from days ago rang sharp in her head. *You're letting him get too close.*

Her sister was right. If Lily kept on this trajectory, she might get her heart broken all over again. *Until we get to the end of this trail and I go back east.* His words from days ago slipped into her consciousness. A reminder that he had never intended to remain in Oregon after herding those cattle across the prairie. Maybe Matt wouldn't die tragically like Harry had, but he would leave regardless.

The best thing she could do right now was keep to herself, figure out how she was going to take care of a baby, how she was going to take care of herself once she reached Oregon.

It was the only safe choice for her heart.

Chapter Ten

THE GRAY CREEP of dawn seeped through frost-laced pines, a pale shroud over the silent camp. The crisp air stung Coop's exposed skin with its icy edge. He crouched low behind Maddie's wagon, the rocky ground biting his knees, a stack of crates draped with a tattered blanket hiding him from the view of the woods.

He barely dared to breathe. A few settlers stirred; their muffled coughs and the clink of a tin cup drifted softly from the shadows. The bugle was hours off, and he figured this was his best chance to find the mystery girl. He flexed his fingers, stiff from cold, and tilted his head, his ears straining in the quiet.

He'd been watching Maddie's wagon for days. There were sometimes empty plates left out, dirty when the rest had already been scrubbed clean. Once, he'd seen a blanket left over the edge of the wagon's tailgate.

Maddie was in on it. He'd wager his last coin. She was leaving food for someone—or even hiding the mystery girl.

He'd been close when Braddock had interrupted him and frightened her off; that had been days ago, and Coop hadn't seen hide nor hair of her since. He was still furious with Braddock, confused by the way Alice had shut Coop down when he had pressed about any kind of friendship between her and the rich snob.

A soft crunch snapped his head up—footsteps, faint on the frost-covered leaves in the woods. Blood rushed loud in his ears, but Coop did his level best to keep his breathing even and quiet.

The steps drew closer, soft and slow, cautious. Was this her? Or someone who had snuck away from camp to find a makeshift privy out in the woods? Fabric swished. He caught a glimpse of a dark-colored skirt from beneath the wagon. And then she stepped into view, one foot on the tailgate step, still cloaked in shadows.

He slid out from his spot, rising slowly, his boots scuffing the ground as he unfolded his stiff limbs. He kept his hands outstretched in front of him to show her he meant no harm as he took a cautious step forward.

The gray light had lifted just enough, and her face happened to be turned toward him. Time stretched slow, every detail sharpening as the world fell away. Her pale skin glowed faint in the dawn, sharp cheekbones, dark hair spilling wild—not in a braid or pulled behind her head. Her eyes were wide and deep, scared the second she caught sight of him.

His chest locked, caught breathless by her beauty. He couldn't look away.

And then time snapped back. She was crouched on the tailgate step, poised with her knees bent, ready to flee. The blade of a small knife clutched in her fist glinted in the rising sun. Where had she drawn it from?

Words tore out before he could catch them. "Hey. I'm Coop—Coop Spencer. I'm not here to hurt you. I swear." He took a half-step closer, his voice cracking as he spoke. He sounded like he was a teenager again, tongue tripping over itself.

She still looked like she was ready to bolt—or maybe to stab him. Her wide eyes darted over him as her breath quickened.

"You saved me, didn't you? I was—I was drunk as a skunk; you hauled me out of that creek. Do you remember?" He swept his hat off his head, but the movement made her jump. He hadn't meant to frighten her.

Her eyes were locked on him, still wide. Her grip tightened on the knife. She stayed silent, and his throat went dry.

"My brother Collin is married to Stella—Maddie's sister. They know me. I'm not a danger." He gestured faintly toward the camp, his hand dropping as he took a small step back.

Her face stayed a blank mask. As she shifted her weight, the tailgate creaked under her. She showed no recognition at his mention of Maddie or Stella. Was Maddie her only connection with the camp?

The quiet stretched between them, heavy and thick—

A shove jarred his shoulder, and Maddie was there, pushing him a few steps back as she planted herself between him and the mystery woman. She squared her shoulders, faced the slender young woman, her stance protective.

"It's all right, Belle—Coop's just a big fool." Her voice was low but firm. She shot a scathing glare over her shoulder.

Belle. The name sank into his heart, soft and beautiful.

Maddie touched Belle's wrist, and her body jerked slightly as she flinched. The knife quickly disappeared into a fold of her shawl. Or a pocket? She'd moved so quickly he hadn't seen.

It was only as the rising dawn spilled over them that he realized her dress was of a shiny material, threadbare and ripped at its bottom hem. It looked like something a saloon girl might wear, cut low until she wrapped a tattered shawl tighter around her shoulders.

His thoughts spun so fast he couldn't seem to catch them. She was clearly frightened—a runaway? Hiding. And Maddie knew about it.

Maddie still faced the girl, speaking in a reassuring tone. "Coop won't tell a soul you're riding in this wagon. Will you, Coop?" Her stern tone dared him to disagree.

He had no intention of doing that. He spoke solemnly. "I swear it, Maddie. Belle. I won't breathe a word." *I just want to talk.*

Belle's eyes flicked to him and then quickly away, her head moving slightly as she glanced toward the wagon, her shawl slipping as she shifted her weight. Then she scurried up into the shadows beneath the canvas. She hadn't spoken a word—not to Maddie and not to him.

He stared after her, something inside him aching to hear her voice. Was it as pretty as she was?

He wanted to know her story. Hadn't even gotten a real chance to say thank you.

Maddie spun toward him and yanked his arm, drawing him a few steps away. Her voice was as hard as iron. "I don't know why you were skulking around here, but Hollis knows she's riding with us. She ran from a bad situation—thinks someone might be after her, trying to drag her back where she doesn't belong."

Hot anger sliced inside him as he thought about the girl he'd really only gotten a glimpse of being trapped in a bad situation, being scared enough that she wouldn't speak to him.

"What's she running from?" He searched Maddie's face.

Maddie shook her head. "I've told her no one is going to chase her all the way out into the wilderness, but she's scared half to death. You leave her alone, you hear me?"

She waited for the nod that he didn't want to give, and then stalked off with one more glare over her shoulder.

Camp was waking up now—more people talking, the scratch of flint on steel, someone making a fire. He didn't have a choice but to walk away. He turned slowly, his hands shoving into his pockets as he trudged back to his own camp, his shoulders hunching against the cold. Someone as scared as Belle had been—scared enough to draw her knife—wasn't going to be easy to approach. He glanced over his shoulder, his gaze lingering on the wagon as a pang of resolve tightened his chest.

Maddie had warned him off, but he still owed a debt to the beautiful, frightened woman inside that wagon. Belle had saved his life. He intended to repay that. Even more so now he knew where she was hiding, knew that she was afraid.

Surely he could find some way to let her know he wasn't a threat. He glanced back once more, his pulse thrumming with purpose.

Lily trudged alongside Stella's wagon. Evening was starting to fall, and every muscle in her body ached. The company— the half of their company that now looked to Leo for leadership—had pushed at a fast pace all day, covering a number of miles on the difficult mountain terrain.

Lily couldn't tell if the aches in her body were from the difficult pace or from the ordeal she'd suffered yesterday.

They had pushed so hard that after a short break to eat something in the afternoon, she had reorganized the crates in the wagon so there was just enough room for Blossom and Alex, and convinced the boy to keep the calf calm.

Now she heard Leo's whistle, his signal for the wagons to circle up.

Mountains rose craggy on either side of this narrow valley, and the lengthening shadows seemed to loom like silent threats. Or maybe Lily was overly sensitive after the warnings they had been given.

With only half the company to make a small circle of wagons, how would they have enough men to stand on watch? Shouldn't they have caught up with the rest of the company by now?

There was the usual activity as the wagons circled up. Lily went to help Alex out of the wagon, and then he helped her set Blossom on her own four legs. The calf bucked and ran in a small circle, oblivious to the tension of the travelers. Even Alex seemed to realize that these weren't normal circumstances as he glanced around cautiously in the gathering dusk.

A rider on horseback circled around the side of camp. As he passed between two wagons, Lily recognized Matt.

She quickly jerked her gaze away, focusing on the calf and the boy. She helped Alex pour milk into the makeshift udder, and he set to feeding the calf. In need of a distraction, she went back to the wagon to straighten things up.

Last night, it had seemed so clear that she should distance herself from Matt, protect her heart from any further hurt. But earlier today, when he passed by on horseback, rifle in hand, she had seen the smile that bloomed on his face as he approached her and Paul and Alex walking near the wagon. She was the one who had averted her gaze without returning his smile, but not before she saw the flash of hurt he quickly masked.

She had seen him again when the pioneers stopped for a

quick bite in the afternoon, and he hadn't even glanced her way. He must've felt her rejection from that morning.

Now she felt even more muddled than she had last night lying alone in her tent.

A series of three sharp whistles rang out through the quiet evening. Alex looked up curiously, and then Maddie was there, motioning for Lily to join her.

"Alex, Paul is with Jenny in the center of camp. Why don't you bring Blossom over and feed her near your brother?"

When Lily joined Maddie, her sister said, "Leo wants a meeting with all the men and women."

Unease trickled through Lily as she drew her shawl tighter around her shoulders and joined a cluster of men circled around Leo. Out of instinct, she began counting heads, tracking that everyone was where they were supposed to be. August stood with arms crossed, face angled out into the darkness, a muscle jumping in his cheek. His wife, Felicity, stood beside him, face drawn in an expression of concern.

There was Stella—but where was Collin?

Everyone whispered until Leo whistled sharply once more.

Lily's chest tightened when she caught Matt's eyes. He stood almost directly across from her. He frowned and quickly looked away, leaving her with her heart pounding in her chest, a memory of yesterday's kiss flaring hot inside her.

"We missed a turn or a cutoff somewhere." Leo's voice rang above the noise, and the crowd instantly went quiet, listening. "We should've caught up with the rest of the company by now. Collin rode back to see where we might've missed a split in the trail." He jerked one thumb over his shoulder.

No wonder Stella had frown lines etched around her eyes and mouth. Even Leo looked worried. Had Collin been the one to volunteer to ride off into a dangerous situation? August flinched at the words and slipped from the circle. Lily wasn't close to him or Felicity, but she had heard Collin's whispered concerns to Stella one night by the campfire. August had been the company scout, one of the best according to Hollis. Until he had lost his sight weeks ago on the trail.

"There's a chance that whoever is out there hunting us might've obscured the trail." Leo's words kicked up a murmur in the crowd, and he waited with a stony stare until they were silent again. "We want everyone who's able to stand watch tonight. We'll take turns, men and women. Everyone armed."

A shiver racked Lily, and when her eyes lifted again, Matt was staring straight at her. This time, the hardness that had been in his gaze earlier was gone, and she seemed to read compassion, concern in his expression. Weary, she looked away this time.

Leo gave a few more instructions, and then the cluster of pioneers broke apart, everyone scattering to their wagons to pull out their weapons.

Maddie locked her arm through Lily's as they made their

way back toward the children. "You've been quiet today. You all right?"

Lily gave a tight-lipped nod.

"I encouraged Stella to make up with you. I don't suppose you'd be willing to say sorry?"

Maddie had always been the peacemaker of the trio. She'd comforted Lily when they had both been young, often urging Stella to find a compassionate bone in her body when she got too bossy.

"Perhaps." Lily's lame murmur. She caught a glimpse of the children; their play wasn't as lighthearted as she'd seen before. Even though they seemed able to read the tension of the adults around them, they were happy, safe.

"You'll be a good mother, Maddie," she said. "You are great at helping those children find their way through an argument."

Maddie wrinkled her nose.

"Remember when we were nine?" Lily asked. The memory brought a hot knot to her throat. "I can't—I can't remember the exact details—but didn't Mary from three doors down trip me and make me spill my lunch pail in the mud?"

Maddie nodded, her eyes alight with the memory.

"They called me names." Lily shook her head. "I ran into the tenement, ran to Pa, crying my eyes out. He just sat in his chair, staring at the wall. He didn't even say a word of comfort. But you came into the apartment, gave me half of your own lunch. And not long after that you sewed me a dress so pretty it made them all jealous." The memories floated up. "But a few days later, I saw Mary's mama bandage a cut on her hand, kiss her forehead tenderly. It hit me hard—I didn't have that."

"We all missed Ma, once she was gone."

"It was more than that," Lily whispered. "Sometimes it feels like everybody leaves me."

Maddie squeezed Lily's arm. "I'm with you always, to the end of the age." Lily knew the Bible verse was from one of the later chapters of the book of Matthew. Maddie had quoted it to her often in their childhood, in those dark days after Ma had passed away. Lily hadn't thought about that in years.

"I know things are changing," Maddie said. "But no matter where we end up once we reach Oregon, I'll still be your sister. I'll do everything I can to help you and that wee one of yours. And you've got a God who loves you and will never leave you."

The words battered at Lily's soul. Her voice cracked when she spoke. "I still needed a father."

Maddie pulled her into a hug, no further words of comfort. Maddie had suffered the same childhood Lily had. All three of them had made the best of a difficult situation. Maddie had been the mother that Lily had never known; she'd done the best she could.

The children called out for Maddie, and Lily pushed back gently. She gave a wet half-laugh and wiped her damp cheeks. "Go take care of your children."

As Maddie walked off, Lily caught sight of Matt once

more as he strode through the edge of camp. He had been watching her but quickly cut his face away.

She'd hurt him with her rejection this morning, but she'd been afraid of letting her heart get involved.

A memory of days ago, waking warm with his coat draped over her, protected from the snowstorm and the cold. Uncertainty plagued her. What was the right thing to do?

* * *

The night was dark, only a hint of moon as it slipped past the horizon behind the mountain. The starry sky stretched overhead like an endless canopy as Matt trudged toward the edge of camp. When Leo had asked him to relieve Lily, Matt wanted to refuse. If he had, it would've caused questions he didn't want to answer.

He felt the sting of her rejection this morning, knew it was because of that kiss, because he'd reached for something that wasn't his to have. He was well aware that she had never accepted his offer of friendship, that she was mourning Harry—the man she'd loved.

It still hurt.

As it was, all he needed to do was trade places with her, send her to her tent for some rest. They barely had to speak. He could bear it for a few moments.

Bright fires burned both inside the circle of wagons and in strategic places outside the circle of wagons, lighting up the whole section of valley. If anyone was trying to sneak into camp tonight, they'd be hard-pressed to find a shadow to hide in.

Lily's slim figure stood straight in between two wagons, a line of tension in her shoulders. The nearest watchman was twenty feet to her left, a vague shape in between wagons, rifle glinting in the firelight.

Matt didn't want to scare her, so he let his footfalls be heavy and loud. She jumped anyway, glancing over her shoulder. The firelight gilded the braid that hung long down her back, strands curling around her face. Her wide eyes and pallor suggested she was frightened at having to stand and keep watch.

For a moment, he forgot his hurt as compassion swelled. She wasn't meant to be holding a rifle like that, wasn't meant to be doing a man's job.

"I'm your relief." He said the words evenly as he drew near.

She nodded and swallowed, her throat moving.

He shouldn't ask, but he blurted, "You all right?"

She nodded again, thrusting the rifle toward him, barrel pointing up into the sky. When his hand accidentally closed over hers on the stock, he realized just how chilled she was. Her fingers felt like small blocks of ice. Protectiveness surged. He wanted to draw her in, embrace her, warm her up.

He forced himself to take a step back.

The easyness they'd shared before was gone. It was his fault. That reckless kiss, a liberty he never should've taken— but one that he couldn't quite bring himself to regret.

An owl hooted in the distance, and she startled. The breeze carried a faint whiff of pine from the woods beyond the camp.

"Me and the other men aren't gonna let anything or anyone come into camp and hurt you," he said.

She still hadn't said a word, and when she looked up at him, he saw the wash of tears in her eyes. Heat clawed at his throat. He shifted his weight, gave her his profile. "I know I'm not worthy to be your friend"—or more—"but I promise I'm not gonna let any harm come to you."

Her brows drew together. She turned to face him fully, her shawl slipping slightly as she clasped her hands in front of her. "Don't say that."

"It's true." He laughed, a brittle sound, more words spilling free. "After my folks died, there was an orphanage for a bit of time." He stared into the darkness beyond the wagons, his jaw tight. "I don't remember much of it now. By the time I was eight, I was a scrawny kid on my own on the streets. One night in the winter—I can still remember the snow piling up—it was bitter cold. I was near frozen, belly clawing itself empty, huddled by a stoop, thinking I'd die there." He kept his eyes fixed on the horizon, shame flooding him, aware that she hadn't gone off to bed, that she was still listening to him.

He kept on. "I was about to fall asleep. Only later realized that if I had fallen asleep, I would've died out there. This young woman shook me awake. She was pretty, had kind eyes, probably sixteen or seventeen. I don't even know what she was doing out there. She helped me to my feet, and I thought for sure she was gonna take me to jail. Instead, she took me to a warm room. Her father's office, I think."

He shook his head, remembering how fine that building had been, how elegant the chair and desk. How he'd sunk into leather cushions that felt like butter on his skin. "The office was... well, I've never seen anything so well-appointed. She plied me with bread and soup, wrapped me in a blanket. It was the first kindness I'd felt in years. I'm not sure I even chewed that bread, but I do remember looking around and wanting to be just like the man who worked in that room. A man with an office like that had to be wealthy enough that he wouldn't wonder where his next meal was gonna come from."

He cleared his throat. His gaze darted to the distant firelight flickering through the wagons, then dropped to the ground. "I heard her talking in the next room. She begged her father to help me, asked him to find me a job or at least send me away with some money. But her pa had taken one look at me and knew that I wasn't worth the dirt on the bottom of his shoes. He said as much. An hour later, I was back on the street, though she made sure I left with that blanket."

A shadow moved, and he turned to stare into the dark. Must've been a branch swaying in the breeze.

When he glanced back at Lily, he found her staring at him, her eyes steady and wide. Compassion was etched on her expressive face. "I can't believe how much you've endured, but I can see God working in your life. 'He led you through that dark valley, set you by still waters,'" she said softly.

He recognized the verse from something Rusty had quoted at him.

He couldn't bear the softness in her eyes, not when she wasn't meant for him. He turned his head, his throat tight. "That businessman was more right than he knew." He couldn't admit to more, couldn't reveal his connection with the Byrnes brothers, not when she was looking at him like this.

"I'm not sure God would want a sheep like me," he murmured.

The old ache throbbed inside him. A faint crackle of a nearby fire underscored the silence. He opened his mouth to send her on to bed when she stepped closer, her chin firm.

"God does want a sheep like you," she said, her eyes sparking with determination. "And I'd be blessed to have a friend like you, too. I never answered you the other night, but I do want to—I want us to be friends."

That hot knot rose in his throat all over again. He should refuse her friendship. She didn't know the truth about him, and she deserved far more than anything he could offer her. Even if last night he'd determined that he would protect her no matter the cost.

But as he stared at her earnest face, so dear to him now, the words to refuse her offer of friendship didn't come. "I'd like that," his traitorous mouth whispered instead.

Her smile was beautiful to behold. "Good."

"Good." He tipped his head toward the wagons. "You'd better get some sleep."

"All right. Good night."

He let his, "good night," echo hers and watched as she carefully made her way into camp. Then forced himself to look out at the night.

What was he doing?

He'd never had anyone claim him like she had, never had anyone take care of him or fight for him.

Rusty had preached at him for weeks, but Matt wasn't sure that he was worth saving. Because if he was Lily's friend—her true friend—he would tell her the truth.

Yet he'd started to want more than friendship. But how could he have that unless he revealed everything?

And if he admitted to his original purpose in following her and her sisters out here on the trail, she would hate him.

Chapter Eleven

THE MORNING SKY stretched pale and thin over the mountains. A crisp bite was in the air, and Matt shifted in his saddle as he rode near the center of the snaking wagon train. Leo was pushing them at a fast clip this morning, determined to catch up with the rest of Hollis's company.

Leo had informed the company this morning that he had sent the cattle on with Lucky and Gerry to herd them, along with a seventeen-year-old boy from the company. The cattle would be difficult for three men alone to herd, but Leo and Collin figured that whoever was hunting them for that ruby would leave the animals alone. It was a gamble, one that Matt hoped would pay off.

His gaze slid to Lily, walking alongside the Fairfax wagon, holding Jenny on her hip. Alex and Paul were herding little Blossom, along with a little girl Matt recognized. He didn't know her name. He couldn't hear what the kids were saying, but they were chattering and gesturing.

Only every once in a while, Paul glanced up with concern marked on his expression.

Lily seemed to be in charge of the children for the time being, but from what he could see, she was distracted, glancing around at the woods and hills around them.

After what had passed between them last night, his heart raced at just the glimpse of her. Her offer of a chance for friendship changed everything. The secret he carried was still unshared, but this morning he'd woken wondering if he needed to admit to what had sent him on this journey. But perhaps he didn't have to come clean. He hadn't taken any action against the Fairfax family, had only listened and tried to put together information. That wasn't a crime, was it?

Collin rode through the company, stopping to talk to someone ahead of Coop's position riding a dozen yards in front of Matt. Most of the men carried their rifles; those on horseback had them across their laps, while men who walked carried them at their sides. Everyone was on high alert.

Collin rode up to join his twin, speaking urgently.

For the first time, Coop didn't seem to be angry with his brother. He seemed to be listening with half an ear while continually glancing at one of the wagons. Whose wagon was it? Maybe Maddie and Jason's? Collin seemed to be on an urgent mission and didn't notice Coop's distraction. He finished with Coop and then rode at a fast clip toward Matt.

"Everything all right?" Matt asked.

Collin reined in, letting his horse come beside Matt's. He sent an eagle-eyed glance at the hilltop to their south. "I found the cutoff late last night," he said. There was a grim set to his mouth. "Seems like there's more than one person out there following us. At least two sets of footprints. Coupla horses. Whoever it is, they dragged in brush and knocked over some rocks to block off the trail—disguised it so it wasn't easy to see."

"They wanted us separated from the rest of the company." The realization slipped from Matt's lips the moment it hit.

Collin nodded, his grimness increasing. "There are too many hiding places out here," he said. "I don't like it. They could be behind any rock or tree waiting to ambush us."

"If there are only two of them, surely we can outgun them."

Collin's eyes darted toward his wife riding that big black closer to the front of the wagon train. "One shot is too many."

Matt imagined bullets flying toward those kids, toward Lily. Collin was right. "Is there any way we can track them?" he asked.

"If August still had his sight, yes. He was the best tracker I ever saw—Hollis said so, too. If he couldn't find whoever's out there, and neither could Hollis, I don't think any of us have a chance at finding them."

Matt didn't want to be stuck waiting, the danger out there unknown.

An illegible shout broke through the woods. Heads turned as something—someone—ran from a copse of pine trees. It was a woman—Irene?—hair wild and tangled, dress tattered. She was running right toward Lily and the kids.

Collin and Matt urged their horses into motion as Collin whistled an alert to the other men. Collin angled his mount straight toward the madwoman waving her arms and heading for the wagon train. Matt raced toward Lily and the kids, intending to put himself between them and Irene.

"Stop!" Irene's shout rang shrill. He couldn't understand her other words. Collin shouted at her.

Coop raced toward his brother. "Get her!"

Matt ran his horse in front of Lily and the kids, jumped off, rifle at the ready, and turned in time to see Collin fly off his horse and toward Irene, who didn't fire a shot but swung one hand through the air. Collin jumped back, and Matt realized the flash of sunlight off metal meant she had a knife. Where was the gun she'd had before?

Collin seemed determined to subdue her and moved in again. Then the boys ran toward Irene, almost as if they were one person, arms raised and yelling at the top of their lungs. Matt diverted, running to intercept them.

Irene's knife slashed toward Collin, but Coop's horse darted between them. Irene fell to the ground. Collin jumped on top of her, hands capturing both her arms. Coop stood over him, looking down. "You got her under control?"

Matt held Paul, Coop held Alex. Matt glanced over his shoulder to see Lily wide-eyed, still holding Jenny. The young girl had her face buried in Lily's skirts, sobbing.

Matt turned back to the boys. "What were you thinking?" he demanded.

"She could've taken a shot at you," Coop growled.

Paul looked subdued, but Alex's eyes spit fire. "We wasn't gonna let her shoot Miss Lily or Ben."

Ben. Must be the girl. What kind of name was that for a girl?

Somewhere behind him, Irene was scuffling and spitting. "I ain't here to hurt anybody!"

Matt and Coop urged the boys toward Lily.

She scolded them as well. "Maddie is going to have your hide when she hears you ran out after a madwoman like that."

Lily patted the girl's shoulder, still holding Jenny. Alex was whispering and gesturing to his brother.

"I'm telling you, there's men out there in the woods, waiting for you in that valley." Irene's words rang clear, and Matt met Lily's terror-stricken gaze.

At the same moment, a shot rang out from up ahead. The wagons at the front of the wagon train hadn't known about Irene or the scuffle that had just ensued. They had kept going. Now there were shouts from the men up ahead. Another shot rang out; a clear scream of pain followed.

"Circle up the wagons!" a cry rang down the line.

Ben's sobs grew even louder. Alex and Paul exchanged wide-eyed looks. Lily herded the children toward the wagon. "Stay close. As soon as the wagons get circled, we'll huddle in the middle."

Matt didn't care for that idea at all, sitting there like fish in a barrel, vulnerable to the unseen threat. He mounted up and wheeled his horse in a circle, looking out into the woods, searching for danger. In the background, Irene cackled maniacally.

* * *

A surge of panic clawed at Lily's throat as the shots rang out from the wagon train. The voices shouting carried too many questions. It couldn't be more obvious that they didn't know where their enemies were.

Coop rode off, assisting the wagons to circle up. Those in the front were turning back while those in the back were coming along the side. That meant that the Fairfax wagon—the one Lily had been put in charge of—could stop where it was. The children huddled close, the boys' bravado from moments ago vanished. Their expressions were etched with terror, and she had no comforting words to give them. In a burst of inspiration, she tasked Paul with holding Jenny for a moment.

"What about Blossom?" Ben sobbed.

"Alex, grab her tether; we'll keep her close to us," Lily said. Everyone seemed a bit steadier with a task to complete.

Lily stretched to reach into the back of the wagon and pulled loose the nearest quilt she could find. Now that the oxen were stationary, she crawled under the wagon and quickly tacked up the quilt to some of the mechanisms on its underside. It wouldn't offer any real protection from a bullet flying their way, but it might be more difficult for anyone out there to see her or the children as targets through the scant barrier.

"Come close. Come here." She took Jenny back from Paul, and she and the other three children huddled close by the wagon wheel on the inside of the circle. The creaking of wagons slowed; other women huddled in the center of the wagons with the same terrified expression Lily felt on her face.

Shouts from the men seemed far away. Another shot fired; one answered.

And then things quieted.

Stella rode past the break in the wagons. Her gaze clashed with Lily's. "Everyone all right?"

Lily nodded, swallowing hard. "What about the men?"

She had lost sight of Matt, didn't know who might have ridden forward, who might've been shot.

Stella shook her head.

What did that mean?

Commotion kicked up outside of the ring of wagons. Lily handed Jenny off to Paul. The children looked slightly calmer now as they focused on petting Blossom and telling the calf that everything was all right, though Ben still sniffled and wiped at her nose.

Lily slipped to the break in the wagons, hovering between the two conveyances. Collin had a hold of Irene, the woman's arms behind her back, hands tied, Lily assumed, with a piece of rope. Stella slid off her horse and approached the woman who had caused them all this trouble.

"I tried to warn ya," Irene said.

"You mean, you tried to create a distraction." Stella's voice was as hard as steel.

"I ain't working with them. I don't know who it is. I saw two men out there with rifles—looked like sharpshooters to me. I give up. I'm tired of bein' hungry all the time. Give me some food."

Her order went ignored.

Leo rode up, reining in his horse with a spray of dust, close enough to speak to Collin.

"There's at least two of them out there—maybe more. One of them's a crack shot. We tried to spot where they were and make an attack of our own, but Caleb got winged in the shoulder. We can't get close enough."

"He all right?" Lily asked.

"I think so. Doc's patching him up."

Leo looked grim, swiveling his head in all directions. "Seems like they've stationed themselves on both sides of that little valley. There's no way to make it back to the cutoff without traveling through there."

Collin shook his head, mouth tight. "I scouted it out best I could last night. It's a narrow space. If they're any kind of shot and stationed up on one of those ledges, they could pick us off easy."

Leo wheeled his horse so he was facing the direction they'd come from this morning. "We don't know what's ahead that way. They could be driving us into a dead end. We need to get back to Hollis and the rest of the company, but the only way is through that valley."

Irene cackled low while staring at Stella, her eyes calculating.

"Why don't we just give them the ruby?" Lily hadn't

meant to blurt out the words. All four heads turned in her direction. There was nothing for it but to finish the thought. "Why not hand it over? Then they'd leave us alone."

Stella shook her head. Lily bristled at her refusal to even listen.

"She ain't know what men like those are about," Irene said to Stella. "She's too soft." She turned her face toward Lily, and the almost wild expression on her features sent a shiver down Lily's back. "It don't matter if you give them the jewel. Men like that will shoot up this entire wagon train just because you've caused them trouble."

Lily's mouth dropped open. It couldn't be true.

But Leo looked grave. "We can't risk it. There's too many women and children among us. We can't put folks in danger like that."

Oh.

"Did you put up that quilt?" Leo directed this question at Lily.

She nodded.

"Good thinking. Makes it harder to see underneath the wagon."

She felt a small stirring of pride. It seemed far too little, too scant a protection when so many lives were at stake out here.

Ben's wailing became louder, and Lily left the tableau to go to the girl, who had collapsed on the ground next to Blossom.

"She just started crying," Alex said, eyes wide and palms upturned.

Paul was rocking Jenny slightly. The littlest girl was growing red in the face, and Lily could only hope that she wouldn't start crying, too. It would be easy for someone to hear and figure out where the children were.

Lily knelt next to the sobbing girl and put a hand on her shoulder.

"It's just—" Ben sniffled—"like it was before. They're gonna kill us all."

"It's not gonna be like that," Lily said.

She wished Felicity were here to comfort the girl. But Ben's adoptive mother was driving another wagon, might even be aiming a rifle in defense right now. Rachel was also close to Ben, but Owen and Rachel had been pushed ahead with Hollis's half of the company. Lily only knew snatches of what had happened to Ben early on in this journey. The little girl had been part of a wagon train massacred by bandits in an attempt to steal all of their belongings. Only Ben and Rachel had survived.

"We ain't gonna let nobody get to you," Alex said fiercely. "Me and Paul been talking about making a slingshot. Pa taught us how to shoot with it."

"That's a right fine idea," Lily said. The boy puffed up with pride.

She knew there was little chance that any of the men hunting them would get close enough for the boys to actually be able to use a slingshot, but if the thought comforted Ben, why not allow for it?

At that moment, Lily glanced up, and her eyes connected with Matt, on his horse outside the circle of wagons. He had his rifle at the ready, though pointed at the ground. There was a fierce look in his expression. He nodded to her, eyes grave and mouth set in a line.

He'd promised that he wouldn't let anyone hurt her. Could she believe him? What if he got himself shot? What if Stella or Maddie got killed?

Panic rose into Lily's throat. She pulled her glance away from the man and looked back at the children, who seemed to be waiting on her. She took a moment to breathe the way Maddie had taught her, shown her again days ago.

"We don't know what's gonna happen," she told the kids quietly, "but we can pray for God's protection right now." That seemed to settle them somewhat, and she started off an awkward prayer.

But the longer she spoke to her Heavenly Father, the more settled she felt in the depths of her soul. Ben's hand snuck into hers. Lily peeked open her eyes to see the others. Paul leaned in close on her other side, Jenny still in his arms, his other hand outstretched to hold Alex's hand.

Peace stole over her, a quiet calm amid the storm. She still felt anxious about what was to come—the possibility of losing someone that she cared about—but in this moment, she leaned into the comfort of a Heavenly Father she knew she could trust.

Chapter Twelve

LILY WAITED with Maddie and the children—Paul, Alex, and Ben. Maddie had Jenny wrapped in a blanket attached to her midsection so that she had one hand free.

She was terrified about what they were about to do, but Leo and Collin and the men had come to the decision that this was the best course of action. The plans had filtered through the group late in the afternoon, as dense clouds had covered the evening sky, obliterating the sunset. Now, the night was dark and close. No hint of moon. There'd only been a sliver of it yesterday anyway.

It was far past the children's bedtime, and they shifted impatiently, seeming to hover on a mix of anticipation, excitement, and fear.

Earlier in the afternoon, the men had attempted to circle around the sharpshooters, only to find themselves shying away from more gunshots aimed right at them. After that failed attempt, things had seemed more dire than ever. Were there two men out in the woods—or more? If the Byrnes brothers thought this jewel was valuable enough to send two men, why not send ten?

No one knew what was waiting out there, but Leo was insistent they had to travel through that valley, get to the cutoff, and do their best to catch up to Hollis and the other wagons. He'd decided that if they moved under the cover of complete darkness, being as silent as possible, they could make it through.

Leo had announced his plan to small groups of settlers, three or four at a time. Was she the only one who had choked back words of refusal? Surely they were going to ride into disaster.

She heard a soft creak, as if the wagon just in front of Stella's wagon had moved off. Blossom was tucked in the back of the wagon, wrapped in a blanket, fed only an hour ago. Lily hoped the calf would simply sleep through this long night.

"It's Matt," came a whisper through the darkness as soft footfalls approached.

"Mr. Matt!" Alex's voice, a mix of excitement and fear. "Time to go?"

"Yes." Matt maintained a whisper. "I know you've already been told, but you've got to stay as quiet as a church mouse."

Lily only had a vague sense of the wagon creeping. Maddie had taken the task of giving the oxen the near-silent command to roll out. Lily didn't know if she'd tapped the lead ox's flank with a stick or what, but the animals were now plodding forward.

Matt still stood close in the darkness. Lily reached out, her fingers finding the cuff of his sleeve. She closed her hand around his wrist for a moment. "Would you stay? Walk with me and Maddie and the kids?"

She hadn't realized how badly she wanted it until the words were there, hastily blurted out. She realized she was still clutching him and let go, only for his big, warm hand to close over hers. There was a moment of brief connection in the darkness, a new awareness flickering between them like a fragile flame. She clung to it, holding on against the dread coiling deep inside her.

"I've got to tell the next wagons to move out. Then I'll be back."

She nodded, which was silly because he wouldn't be able to see her in the pitch blackness.

Ben huddled close, and Maddie let her arm rest around the girl's shoulders. Ben had been subdued all day, still terrified that the men who were hunting that ruby were going to come and attack the wagon train outright. While Lily had helped make a quick lunch, Felicity and August attempted to console the girl. But Felicity needed to drive her wagon and had asked Lily to watch over the girl, tears in her eyes as she had done so.

Walking in the complete darkness was a bit terrifying. Lily jumped at every snap of a twig, every jolt of the wagon rolling hard over a stone.

And then Matt was back, his horse trailing behind him.

He had to be holding the reins. She breathed easier by the fact of his presence, an arm's length away.

The boys bickered in faint whispers. Maddie, on their other side, shushed them. But it was Ben who let out a hiccup that sounded like the prelude to a sob.

"We have to stay quiet, remember?" Lily whispered to the little girl. "What about a guessing game?"

"I'll go first." Paul. It was strange to hear the disembodied voice come from the darkness. "I'm tall when I'm young, short when I'm old. What am I?"

"A tree," Alex guessed softly.

Maddie shushed them again, though Lily didn't think their small whispers had carried far.

"A candle," Ben whispered, barely audible.

"That's right," Paul said. "Your turn next."

Lily didn't hear Ben's riddle, but the boys must have because they whispered rapid-fire guesses. She wasn't sure that her suggestion of a game was the best idea, but the children seemed to find the distraction they needed in it.

They'd gone several paces when she felt the choking fear start to rise in her throat. Then Matt edged closer, and his hand closed over hers, warm and sure.

Her breath stuttered once in her chest, then rushed out in a long exhale, some of her tension with it. He squeezed her hand gently. Her shoulder brushed his muscled arm before she figured out how to adjust her stride to his.

"Do you have a guess, Mr. Matt?" Alex prompted quietly from the darkness. They must still be stumped on Ben's riddle.

"Can't say that I do. I don't think I've ever played this game before."

It was her turn to squeeze his hand. She felt a beat of tension in him, and then a slight relaxation, as if he had accepted that she would know that the things he had missed from his past could still be painful for him.

"Maybe it's time for another game," Maddie whispered when the children became restless.

"I don't wanna play," Alex said, suddenly serious.

"I'm scared," Ben's voice rang out in the sudden stillness between them.

There was a bit of silence. Lily didn't have another idea. She was as terrified as the children.

And then Matt spoke. "I've got something that might help."

He let go of her, and she had the sense of his arm moving, as if he had reached inside his pocket. She heard a faint clinking sound, and then Matt steadied her with his hand for a step as he moved past her in the darkness; she sensed one arm reaching out for Ben.

"Hold out your hand," Matt ordered quietly. "All of you kids. I'm gonna give you something."

There was a beat of silence, and then Ben's quiet wonder, "It's so tiny. What is it?"

"It's cold," Alex whispered.

"These are little pieces of a watch," Matt explained.

For a moment, her heart banged against her ribcage. He was giving away pieces of his broken pocket watch—the one he'd carried with him all this time?

"I think these pieces are sort of lucky. Nothing bad's ever happened to me when I've been carrying them—nothing I wasn't able to get out of," he amended quietly. "If each of you hold onto them, maybe you'll have that same kind of luck."

There was a chorus of whispered thanks, and then Matt fell into step beside her again, gathering his horse's reins back from her hand.

"That was a real nice thing to do," she whispered to him. She could hear the faint whispers of the children wondering over their new treasures. Matt had kept those pieces for years, and now he'd chosen to share them with the children. The wonder of it warmed her from the inside out.

She thought about Harry for one beat. Would he have been so generous? She hadn't thought about him all day because Matt had begun to take up her thoughts. Matt, whom she looked for across camp; Matt, who was showing kindness.

His hand closed over hers again, drawing her a half step closer to him, protecting her. In that quiet, shadowed moment, she felt tethered to him—not just in friendship but something deeper, a fragile hope that steadied her against the night's uncertainty.

The company emerged from the valley just as the first rays of dawn began to creep over the horizon, casting a faint, golden glow across the weary travelers. It had been a long night, and

Matt felt every hour that they hadn't slept weighing him down to the bone.

Word had come down the line for every man to mount up and take to arms as the sky began to lighten.

He separated from Lily and the kids with great reluctance. He liked the way that she had asked for him, that she had leaned into him when she had been afraid.

Maybe he liked it too much. She had agreed to friendship, had told him once before that she wasn't looking for a husband. But every moment that he spent with her made him long for things that he hadn't allowed himself to want for a very long time.

Now he couldn't help looking for her among the rolling wagons as the company picked up its pace under daylight. The children had been tucked into one of the wagons, hopefully sleeping now. Lily and the other women were cautiously walking alongside the oxen, using the wagons for a shield as much as they possibly could. Surely in this flat expanse where the earth had leveled out, there were fewer places for a man to hide. Fewer places from which he might aim a gun right at the vulnerable pioneers.

Matt hadn't realized that his horse's slow gait had brought him within speaking distance of Irene, whose hands were tied to the back of one of the wagons. She walked along behind it, stumbling occasionally. He knew she'd been fed supper last night. Had overheard Collin saying as much. Now she glared at him, and her eyes narrowed. In recognition? She wore a hawk-like look, as if she were a predator and he the prey.

"Don't I know you?" she asked.

He shrugged, letting his head turn so that his profile faced her. He shifted, nudging his horse so that the animal sped up a half step. But he was still in earshot when she called out to him again.

"I remember you from the docks."

Heat flashed up his spine. He reined in his horse so that when the wagon she was tied to crept forward, he was only a few feet away from her. Her eyes were sharp and calculating. He remembered Lily's statement from before, that she wasn't in her right mind, but right now she seemed sharp as a tack. He had to be very careful what he said.

"What's your name?" she asked.

"You don't need to know that."

She smiled as if he had given her a juicy piece of information. "Which one sent you out here—Amos or his brother?"

When he didn't answer, she said, "I can guess what you're after."

"Not anymore," he said as firmly as he could.

He hadn't meant to let his gaze flick to Lily, several wagons ahead, but when he looked back at Irene, some of the haggardness had disappeared from her face as her lips twisted in a semblance of a smile.

"So that's how it is, eh?"

A sudden bolt of fear twisted into anger in his gut. He inched his horse closer. She flinched back, even though he was still a foot and a half away. "These good people could've hanged you or left you out in the wilderness, tied up for the wolves to feast," he said, voice low. "You should forget all about that ruby and make yourself a new life."

That's what he wanted more than anything else, more than ever: a chance for his friendship with Lily to grow, a chance to win her heart.

He started to move away, but she called out, "You'll never escape their hold." Her words were as sharp as the winter wind from days ago, slicing deep. "You'll never be anything but one of his lackeys, no matter where you run."

Her taunt clawed into him, raking his gut raw.

She was wrong. He could start over. He could be someone new, leave that boy who'd grown up on the streets, the young man who'd worked on the docks in the shadows, telling half-truths and hiding from the authorities. He wasn't that person anymore.

Stella rode her big black right next to him. "What did she say to you?" she demanded.

He hadn't realized she'd been watching. He leaned on every ounce of the practice keeping a straight face when confronted by the authorities in order to wear a blank mask. He shook his head. "A bunch of nonsense."

He only hoped Stella wouldn't ride over to Irene and ask her outright what had passed between them. If there was any time for distraction, this was it.

"I know you don't like me. Don't like my friendship with Lily." There were no two ways about it, not with the way she gave him the cold shoulder, ignoring him if he ever happened to be in her presence. "But Lily misses you. She needs her sister."

For a moment, Stella looked stricken, and then her expression hardened. "It doesn't matter what I think about you."

"It might—to Lily."

She shook her head.

"I'm working on being a man worthy of her." He hadn't meant to make the admission, couldn't tell what she felt as she kept her inscrutable expression.

"Ever read the Bible?" she asked.

Shame threatened to send a flush up his face, but he met her stare head-on. "Can't read. No schooling to speak of. Rusty's been preaching at me for weeks, though."

"That's the place to start. Not to be worthy of Lily, but to be a man redeemed." She gave one tight nod and rode off, leaving him to his tumbling thoughts.

That's what he wanted. To be redeemed, to have his past wiped clean. He hadn't thought it was possible, but now everything Rusty had spoken to him these past weeks whirled like a dervish inside him. Was it really possible to leave the Matt from New York City behind? Start fresh?

A glance over his shoulder showed Irene watching him. She seemed to be laughing to herself, and it unsettled him. Who had spoken truth—Stella, or Irene? Could he outrun the man he'd been?

A single gunshot cracked sharp through the morning, shattering the hushed stillness.

Chapter Thirteen

A SECOND GUNSHOT pierced the quiet, sharp and jarring, followed swiftly by a horse's whinny and a chorus of shouts echoing with urgency, this time from the rear of the convoy.

After their long night of sneaking through that valley, were the men now behind them?

Two wagons from the rear rushed forward. Matt wheeled his horse out of the way as one nearly barreled him over. Whoever was supposed to be tending those wild-eyed oxen was nowhere in sight. Then Matt realized one of the animals was bleeding from a wound in its back leg.

Another gunshot—and someone returning fire.

A desperate cry. And then a shout, "Maddie! I need Maddie or the Doc!"

If men hunting that ruby were behind them, the best thing they could do was try to outdistance them.

Matt gave a frantic glance around the wagons, all now

moving at a faster clip—those two out-of-control wagons already gone from sight. Lily was ahead on foot, in the middle of the convoy. Her shawl was a faint blur through the dust raised by the oxen's hooves and the turning wheels. He knew the kids were inside the wagon. She was jogging beside the wagon, talking frantically up into it. He didn't like her being out in the open.

He was riding to catch up with her, low over his horse's neck, when he heard another shot from a copse of pine trees fifty yards north of their path. Before he could open his mouth to shout, a ragged hole tore through the wagon canvas just above Lily's head.

"Lily, get down!" His shout seemed to dissipate in the melee. Two other wagons at the front of the company sped up. If there was a shooter behind and a shooter at their side, could they outrun the gunshots?

He kept racing toward Lily, glancing at those woods, trying to catch sight of a shirt or pant leg or glint of sunlight off a rifle barrel—anything that would tell him the shooter's location, where he needed to aim his weapon.

When he glanced back at Lily, she was looking over her shoulder at him, her face white with terror. Closer to the wagon now, he could hear Jenny wailing, one of the boys' voices shouting.

There was no sign of Maddie or the Doc. Hopefully they were on horseback, riding to help where they were needed.

Men's shouts carried back wagon to wagon. "There's a valley up ahead. Turn off!"

Matt passed the instructions behind him. Maybe the valley would offer some cover.

He'd almost reached Lily when Stella's black bolted into the open, toward the north—toward those woods. Had she spotted the shooter?

He couldn't take the time to look. He needed to get Lily into that wagon.

"Grab hold of me," he called out as he neared her, only slowing his horse slightly. He leaned off the side of the saddle, squeezing tight with his legs, reaching out with one arm. She grabbed for him at just the right moment, and he swept her into his arms.

For a broken moment, he held her close. Thanked the Good Lord that she was safe. Basked in the feeling of her arm coming around his shoulder, her breath warm on his neck.

"The kids are in there!" She was shaking with terror but worried about the kids.

"I'll get you to the wagon seat."

He rode as close to the turning wagon wheels as he dared, wincing when it rolled over a protruding rock and jolted up into the air. Jenny wailed louder.

"Can you grab on to the seat?" he asked.

She was already leaning over. He held her waist as best he could as she made the narrow jump from the horse's back onto the wagon seat. She'd made it! Relief flashed through him.

She gathered up the reins, attempting to gain some control over the oxen.

Beyond the wagon, he saw Stella jerk back in the saddle, saw a spray of red. Stella must've been shot. She tumbled from the saddle. Her horse raced off, but Stella remained on the ground. If whoever was in those trees had hit Stella while she was moving at such a fast pace, they might be able to hit her again where she lay still on the ground.

He didn't know whether Lily had seen—only knew that if her sister died, Lily would be devastated by grief. He slowed enough for the wagon to pass him, and then took off into the open. Over his shoulder, he checked that Lily had gained control of the oxen. Then he saw the first couple of wagons pass an outcropping of rock.

A boom shook the ground, so loud that it roared through his chest. Rocks crashed down from the outcropping, sliding from the mountainside in a thunderous cascade, covering the trail ahead with jagged debris. Only the cutoff into that narrow valley was left.

The first two wagons had bolted ahead of the rockslide; the next one in line tried to make the turn, veering so strongly that for a moment it was on two wheels. The momentum of the oxen gained control, and it slammed back down onto the ground. The other wagons followed into the narrow valley.

Matt turned back. He raced toward Stella, loosening one foot from the stirrup and then jumping from the horse's back while it was still moving forward. He tumbled to the ground, jarring his shoulder.

He whistled for the horse to come back, relieved when he saw its hooves kick up dirt as it rapidly turned. He had made it. He ran the last two steps to Stella and scooped her over his shoulder. She moaned. Blood flowed slick from her body down his shoulder. He staggered to his feet, her weight slowing him. With one arm holding her on his shoulder, he gripped the saddle horn with the other.

He had one foot in the stirrup when hot pain sliced through his opposite shoulder. The force of it knocked him back, but he gritted his teeth and slung himself into the saddle, kicking his horse before his feet were in the stirrups. He held onto Stella as tightly as he could, realizing that his left hand was almost useless.

The valley was just there—only a dozen yards ahead. He pushed his horse for more speed, leaning over the saddle as best he could, ready for a bullet to cut through his back.

* * *

Coop was off his horse, helping an older woman who had stumbled, when an out-of-control wagon raced past them. He supported the woman with one hand under her elbow and boosted her into her wagon, pressing the oxen reins into her hands before he glanced around to see whether anyone else needed help.

In the chaos of gunshots and shouts and terrified screams, it was hard to tell what was what.

Another out-of-control wagon careened straight toward him. He jumped out of the way, recognizing Rob's wagon as it passed—and Rob inside, shouting commands to try to gain control of the oxen.

Right behind it, coming just as fast, was another wagon.

Wait. That was Maddie's wagon! At the instant of recognition, a flash and an explosion so strong the ground shook nearly sent him to his knees.

The two wagons narrowly escaped the falling rocks cascading down from the side of the mountain. Coop jumped into his saddle, a tug pulling him toward Maddie's wagon. Belle was hiding inside. He was certain of it, though he hadn't caught sight of her again after that morning three days ago.

She must be terrified. And what if the wagon crashed into something in the oxen's panicked run?

He raced past Leo, who shouted, "Coop, leave the wagons!"

And when Coop ignored his brother, Leo shouted, "Stop!"

Coop kicked his horse. "Ha!" He saw the two out-of-control wagons round a bend in the trail and leaned over his horse's neck for more speed.

He felt a pang for leaving his brother behind, but Belle needed help, too—and he owed her a life debt.

Maddie's wagon bounced dangerously on the rutted trail. He could imagine what might happen if the wagon lost a wheel.

What if he could catch her attention, get her to open the back of the canvas, have her jump free? The road narrowed, rock walls looming close.

"Hey!" he shouted. He'd almost come even with the wagon, but now his horse couldn't get past. He reined in strongly, his horse bending its back legs as it tried to pull to a stop. Coop's leg scraped against the rock wall as hot pain flared through his thigh. But the wagon was clear.

He spurred his horse for more speed. Some kind of metal piece fell loose from the wagon. As it came at them, Coop's horse jumped. He held onto the saddle and grunted as the amazing animal gave chase.

The shots were fainter now that there was some distance between them and the dust-up back behind. Coop had the wind in his ears, and each stride of the horse thudded into the ground as they gained on the wagon again. He could barely see Rob's wagon up ahead. Maddie's wagon still rocked dangerously. He finally pushed for enough speed to get around it, shouting commands for the oxen to stop.

They didn't listen, lost to their terror. Then he saw Belle attempting to crawl over the front of the wagon, trying to reach the reins.

"Hold on!" he called out to her. She didn't make any acknowledgment that she'd heard him.

Rob's wagon finally began to slow ahead, but Maddie's surged forward. And then he saw the boulder looming, massive and dug deep into the ground.

"Gee!" He shouted the command for the oxen to turn to the right, used his horse in line with the nearest ox's shoulder to try and push the animals to the right so the wagon would not hit the massive rock.

The wagon tilted, wood and metal groaning under the strain, and for a heartbeat, he thought they'd cleared the obstacle. Until one of the back wheels slammed into the boulder, a sickening crunch splitting the air with splintering loudness.

Coop reined in, urging his horse to round, and hopped off. Belle was slumped inside, her cry swallowed up by the canvas.

A glance over his shoulder showed that Rob's wagon had come to a complete stop. His oxen were snorting, heads dipped low. Coop let his focus return to Maddie's wagon. Belle lay crumpled behind the seat, crates toppled in a jagged heap around her.

His chest burned, both with fear for her and relief that the wagon had finally stopped.

Coop stepped onto a broken wheel, tugging at the edge of the canvas closest to him.

"Belle?" He asked the question quietly, not daring to reach for her. He knew she was breathing because he could see the rise and fall of her shoulder. Her dark hair tangled across her face. Her hand slipped beneath her shawl. When it came back into sight, that knife was gripped in her white-knuckled fist.

Maddie's warning echoed through his mind. He didn't try to get any closer.

"Are you all right?" He glanced behind the wagon, in the direction they'd come from. There was no sign of other riders or wagons. Had the others from their caravan been trapped by that rockslide? There had been a valley back there cut into the side of the mountain, he was certain of it. He didn't know if his brothers were all right, but he couldn't go to them. Not yet.

He leaned back slightly, glancing at the wrecked wagon, spoke to her quietly again. "The wagon's done—the wheel's busted clean through." There would be no salvaging Maddie and Jason's wagon this time.

He waited for some movement from her. Anything. "If someone's coming after us, horseback's quicker. We can outrun them."

Now she looked up at him, her eyes wide and searching.

"I'm not going to let anyone hurt you."

She moved slowly, favoring her left side as she pushed to a seated position.

His eyes fell to that knife again. "Do you wanna put that down?"

She shook her head slightly. The first answer she'd given to anything he'd said.

"All right."

She started to stand, ready to clamber over the seat. Instinctively, he reached for her. She flinched away, and his gut twisted. He quickly moved back, stepping off the wheel and hovering in case her legs went weak or she needed help.

At the same moment her feet hit the ground, she shrank behind him. He turned to see Rob approaching. The other man strode closer, even as Coop put himself fully between Braddock and Belle.

"We've got to get back. Alice and the rest of your family are trapped back there!" Rob jabbed a finger toward the valley, boots planted wide.

The knot in Coop's gut tightened. He clenched his fists, stepping closer. He had hated leaving his sister behind, but they didn't know how many men were out there shooting at them.

"They rigged some kind of explosion—we don't know how many guns are out there," he argued back. "I say we ride for Hollis, get more help."

He was aware of Belle, small and trembling, behind him. In his peripheral vision, he saw her shrink against the wagon, head turning toward the shadowed trees like she was going to run.

Braddock's eyes glanced behind Coop. His eyes narrowed as he took a step forward. "Who's that?"

"None of your concern." Coop shifted to block Rob's view.

Rob bristled, eyes sparking fire. "We can't just leave the others."

Coop's temper snapped. "You think you're so smart, Mr. Fancy Pants, but if we ride back there, we might get ourselves shot. Our best choice is to go to Hollis."

"My horse is gone," Rob said, his voice low and clipped. "The rope must've snapped."

"Then we'd better get a move on." Coop reached for the horse's reins. "She'll ride the horse. We can cut through harder terrain on foot and with the horse."

Rob looked like he wanted to argue, but maybe something Coop had said made sense because he finally gave in with a growl, stomping toward the woods, leaving Coop and Belle to follow. Belle flinched at the sound, huddling closer to the horse, her breath hitching softly.

"We've got to go," he said quietly. And then she let him help her into the saddle.

* * *

Lily couldn't stop shaking. She couldn't find the air to breathe. Her lungs didn't seem to be working right. The oxen were pulling the ragged wagon at a pace fast enough to make her teeth rattle.

There were screams, including those from the children inside the wagon, gunshots firing without any pattern.

She had seen Stella fall, had seen the spray of blood.

She'd glanced over her shoulder a second time to see Matt dive off his horse. And then the oxen had followed the next wagon through the narrow mouth of the valley, and she had lost sight of her sister and the man she had come to care about.

Was Stella dead?

The fears that had plagued Lily for the past days seemed to overpower her now and leave her entire body weak.

The wagon jolted as a wheel rolled over an obstruction.

"Where are we going?" Paul's shout broke through the noise in her head, and Lily came to her senses, though her heart felt as if it had left her body. She had to keep the oxen under control, had to put more distance between them and the gunshots still firing behind. There were only three wagons ahead of her, and they had spread out in a meadow between craggy cliffs that rose on either side, making this a basin. Her eyes locked on what lay ahead: gray, blank pits.

Just like those they'd passed in another valley. The same kind of quicksand where Blossom's mother had sunk, never to be seen again.

And these pits were big enough that an entire wagon could sink into their depths.

She pulled on the reins with all her might, bracing her feet against the wagon's box. She gave the command for the oxen to halt, relieved when they started to obey. But the other wagons didn't seem to understand what danger lay ahead.

"Stop!" she screamed. "You have to stop!"

At least one of the wagons heard her because it started to veer to the side. They must've shouted, too, for other wagons began to slow. The white quicksand pit blocked any forward motion. Was there even a path behind them?

The wagon had come to a halt. Hoofbeats echoed from behind. She gripped the revolver that Collin had pressed on her earlier and began to climb down from the wagon box on shaky legs.

"Stay put," she ordered the children.

Ben was sobbing in the wagon bed, Alex and Paul kneeling with wide eyes.

"Take care of Jenny. Take care of each other."

Jenny was squalling on the floor of the wagon bed, and Paul was quick to scoop her up into his arms.

Leo rode in, followed by Collin and what looked to be the last wagon. Where was Matt?

Two more gunshots fired, even as Leo called for the

wagons to circle up. The circle was even smaller now. Had they lost two wagons in the melee?

One last rider appeared; her heart leapt as she dropped the gun gently onto the ground near the wagon wheel. It was Matt, with Stella over his shoulder. As he neared, she saw he was slumped in the saddle—his entire torso covered with blood.

His or Stella's?

Lily started running, only peripherally aware that Collin dismounted from his horse nearby, ran toward Matt. Collin outpaced her and met Matt several yards from the wagons. He reached up and took Stella from Matt's arms. His keen of grief tore Lily's heart.

"Maddie! Maddie!" Only after the words left her mouth did Lily realize she was the one screaming so loudly.

Matt remained slumped in his saddle. Lily knew instantly that he was hurt. She ran past Collin carrying Stella toward the wagons.

Before she could reach Matt, he swung his leg over the horse. When his boots touched the ground, his knees almost buckled. She braced her arm around his waist, freezing when he flinched.

"Where are you hurt?" she asked.

Leo was there, glancing between them before running off to follow Collin and Stella, obviously judging that Matt could stand on his own two feet. "You all right?"

At Matt's terse nod, Leo wheeled his horse. "I need scouts!" Leo roared toward the small circle of wagons.

"Winged me in the shoulder," Matt mumbled.

He was alive. Injured, but alive. Feeling the warmth of him, his weight somewhat leaning into her, tears flooded her eyes. She blinked them back, trying to stay strong.

It hit her as she helped him stagger toward the circle of wagons—their only defense, uncertain as it was: If Matt hadn't come back, if he had been lost, her heart would be broken.

The realization flooded her with emotion. A tear slipped down her cheek, but she didn't let go of him to raise her hand and wipe it away. There was no more guilt. Harry wasn't here anymore. He was gone. And while she'd held affection for him, there hadn't been enough time for it to bloom into real love. Imagining Matt being taken from her brought a wave of grief that threatened to tear her in two.

What she'd thought was friendship growing between them was something more, something sure and certain. Something that felt like falling in love.

As they passed through the narrow space between two wagons, he stopped walking and nudged her so that she turned slightly toward him. Had he felt the sob in her throat? In this closeness, she could see the lines of pain bracketing his face, his mouth. But it was the concern written in his eyes that captured her.

"I'm all right," he said.

She shook her head, afraid if she opened her mouth that sob would break free.

"What about you? What about the kids?" he asked.

"We're all right." Her gaze fell to his shoulder, to the red blood on his shirt seeping down his sleeve. Her tear fell free.

He raised his uninjured arm to brush it away with his thumb. He gently fingered a strand of her hair that had fallen loose, tucking it behind her ear.

Her chin trembled. "I can't believe you went after Stella and got yourself shot."

His voice came low and tender. "Losing your sister would tear you apart. I couldn't let that happen."

Emotion bubbled over. Would Stella survive? She hadn't been conscious from what Lily had seen, and there had been so much blood...

Matt pulled her close with his good arm, and she clung to him, burying her face in his neck as hot tears spilled free. Chaos swirled around them—shouts from Leo as he ordered some of the men to form a line in front of the wagons with rifles ready in case whoever was out there attempted to approach. Jason and Maddie's clipped tones as they worked to save Stella. Another voice—one of the other pioneers—calling out that they were getting a fire going.

This wasn't the time for her to break apart. She took a shuddering breath, attempting to steady herself, edged back from Matt slightly. The grooves of pain in his face had grown deeper.

"Let me get some water, and something to stop your bleeding."

A flare of admiration lit his eyes. She wasn't sure she deserved it, but then remembered his words from days earlier calling her brave.

"I'm so grateful you rode after her," she blurted before she thought better of it. And then, "I care about you, Matt."

A flash of surprise, then warmth in his eyes. There wasn't time for more. She let go of his hand to try and find some water. And she should check on the children. They were probably terrified. They didn't need to see Maddie and Jason working on Stella—or Matt, who also needed the doc's help.

Leo's shout broke into her thoughts. "They've got us well and trapped in this valley. This may be our last stand."

Chapter Fourteen

OUCH. Matt bit back the word, doing everything he could not to flinch at the probe of Doc's metal tweezers poking into the wound on his shoulder. He was shirtless, figured his shirt was ruined with how much blood it'd soaked up. Lily had promised to try and find him another. That was fine—he didn't really want her to witness Doc digging this bullet out of his arm.

It had been well over two hours since Doc and Maddie had worked on Stella. Maddie was still with her sister in a tent that had been quickly erected to keep the sun and wind and dust off their patient.

Jason had come to Matt not long ago, his mouth set in a grim line. When Matt had asked about Stella's condition, Jason had shaken his head slightly.

It wasn't an answer. Would she live?

Matt tried to ignore the pain, to focus on Collin crossing

to the tent, kneeling at its mouth to speak to Maddie. The man had been walking around camp, helping the injured, and trying to help Leo figure out the best plan for defending their little piece of the company—but it was clear he was unfocused, devastated about his wife's injury.

The pain in Matt's shoulder abated for a brief second, and as Jason relaxed his pressure, Matt let out a shaky exhale.

"Any sign of the two wagons that missed the turnoff?" Doc murmured the question before, "I've still got to get the bullet out."

Matt braced for the pain as Doc dug back into his arm. He shook his head to the man's question and then looked up at the sky, trying not to scream at the burst of white-hot pain.

They'd had no sign of Coop Spencer or Rob Braddock. He could only hope they had gone for help.

After Leo's exclamation that they were trapped in this valley, he had sent several men to scout a way around the quicksand pits. That news had come back hopeless—they spread all across the valley floor away from the mouth where the wagons had entered. They had no way around, over, or through them.

The sun was setting now, and Matt was afraid Byrnes's men were going to rush the camp at dark. Their numbers were lower without the other hired hands who had been sent ahead with the cattle, as well as no Coop, no Rob Braddock.

Stella wasn't the only one injured. Some folks had been hurt when wagons had broken loose, oxen out of control. An air of desperation lingered around camp.

There had to be a way out of this.

Leo strode up to Doc, one of the other pioneers shadowing him. "Collin, I need you," he called out. And then to Jason, "We've got to work out some kind of plan."

Collin joined them, Jason listening as he continued to dig the bullet out of Matt.

"Seems like the two men have put themselves in position on either side of the valley where we came in," Leo said. "No matter how we approach, close to the wall or out in the open, they've got a clear shot at us. Wilbur nearly took a bullet."

The man behind Leo nodded.

Matt felt a moment of relief as Jason pulled a piece of metal from his arm and then clamped a cloth over the wound. Every heartbeat felt like a pulse of fire, though Jason had said the bullet had hit him in a lucky spot, the fleshy part of the juncture where his arm met his shoulder.

Matt didn't feel so lucky. But then he thought about Stella, about Lily pressing herself close, and about the words she'd spoken to him. Maybe he was lucky after all.

"What if we abandon the wagons?" Collin said, voice rough. "We take the women and kids and climb up that mountainside and make a run for the rest of the wagons."

Leo looked grim. "Half of us wouldn't be able to get up that mountain. Its slope is so sheer," he said, as if he'd already spent time considering the solution. "August can't see. Stella can't walk. And there's a lot of kids."

Collin's jaw tightened at the reminder of his wife.

"What if we rush them?" Matt offered. "If we took every

man in the company, surely one of us would get a shot that would take them out."

Leo shook his head. "As far as I can tell, both of them are sharpshooters. We'd risk losing too many. Do you wanna ask the wives to send their husbands to get killed?"

He didn't, but they couldn't just wait here to face another attack. Those men out there had planned to send them into this valley where there was no route of escape. That rockslide had pushed the wagons right down this trail. The quicksand meant there was no moving forward, and the sheer cliffs meant there was no way up out of the ravine. They had separated this segment of wagons from the company itself. If they'd gone to this much trouble, who knew what they had planned next?

A commotion kicked up, sounds of a struggle. Jason, who was threading his needle, looked up as Leo and Collin turned to the disturbance.

Another pioneer he thought was named Hank Jordan hauled a man in front of him, someone Matt vaguely recognized from New York City. The man's hands were bound behind his back, and he had a bruise blooming on his cheek. Jordan had a scrape across his jaw, and his hair and clothes were mussed, as if he'd been in a fistfight.

"This good-for-nothing was trying to sneak up on our camp, but he didn't notice me keeping watch. I got the jump on him." Jordan gave the man a shove. He went to his knees on the other side of Leo and Collin. Matt ducked his head, angling himself slightly so that Jason's head and shoulders might block him from view.

"How many others are out there?" Leo demanded.

The man spat on Leo's boot. Leo responded with a kick to the man's midsection.

The man grunted, now lying on his side. "I ain't saying nothing."

Collin leaned down, fisting the man's shirt in both his hands and shaking him. "How many?" he roared.

"I ain't talking," the man repeated. He turned his head slightly, his eyes skittering around, probably looking for an escape. Then his eyes landed on Matt, and they flared recognition.

Jason put a stitch in; the poke of the needle and the pull of the thread made Matt want to howl.

"Well, well. Who we got here?" the man said.

Collin glanced at Matt, his hands still twisted up in the stranger's shirt. Collin's face was red with fury. Matt knew that everything he felt about Stella being injured was at risk of pouring out onto the man's head.

"As I live and breathe, it's Matt Grayson. You're a long way from New York City." The words dropped into a sudden silence.

Jason went still, needle in his fingers while the thread trailed down.

There was motion in the periphery of Matt's vision, but he couldn't seem to look away from Byrnes's man.

"What's he talking about?" Leo demanded.

"We saw you through a pair of field glasses. Figured you were working an inside angle on the ruby."

Collin shoved the man into the ground and wheeled on

Matt, eyes wild. He stayed several feet away, but now all his fury was pointed at Matt. "You work for Byrnes?"

A soft gasp fell into the moment. Matt glanced up. Lily stood several feet away, a bucket of water in one hand, a handful of white fabric in the other. Her face was pale, eyes wide.

She had heard everything.

Lily froze, only her heart beating in her ears, threatening to drown out everything else. She stared at Matt, unable to comprehend what she'd heard.

"Lily," Matt's voice broke on her name. He shifted as if he was going to stand up, but Jason pushed against his shoulder. Matt's knees buckled. Had the doctor known exactly where to press? He sank back to the ground with a sharp grunt, his good hand clawing at the frozen earth for balance.

"I'm putting the last of these stitches in," Jason said seriously. He held the needle at the ready, but a muscle jumping in his jaw indicated he was holding back anger too.

"Irene's gone!" a man's voice shouted from the circle of wagons.

Lily jumped. One hand flew to her chest, pressing against her racing heart.

After Felicity had come to take Ben for the night, she'd left the boys in the wagon, Alex feeding a restless Jenny, Paul worrying over every option of what might happen next.

Panic fluttered in her gut. Surely someone would notice if a madwoman approached the children's wagon. Wouldn't they?

Lily couldn't seem to make her feet move.

Another voice called out, the words indistinct. Leo's expression turned dark as a thundercloud as he glanced from Matt to the man lying on the ground—hands bound—and back to Collin. He raked a hand through his hair, then mashed his hat back on his head.

"I have to go see what happened," he muttered. "Don't kill him," he told his brother. He turned sharply and stalked off.

"Is it true?" Collin demanded, looming over Matt.

Lily wanted to know the answer too.

Matt's head tipped back, as if in pain, as the doctor worked on his shoulder. The fingers of his good hand dug into the ground beneath him. His teeth were gritted as he answered, "It started out that way."

I care about you. The words Lily had said to him hours ago in her storm of emotion burst into her memory. Everything she'd shared with him, everything they had been through...

Had it all been a lie?

"Yes, I came after the ruby. Wanted to find it and leave. I never intended violence on anybody." His voice was rough. His stare pierced Lily, but she couldn't look at him and lowered her face toward the ground. She should leave—just walk away. But she couldn't get her feet to obey.

"You joined up with our company under false pretenses," Collin muttered angrily. "Been lying to us for weeks."

"I don't want the ruby anymore," Matt insisted. "Haven't for a while. Been out here in the wild, getting to know you—" he threw the words toward Lily, even though Collin had been the one speaking to him—"changed me, made me a better man."

She chanced a look up again. His gaze was pleading as he searched her face. When Lily didn't respond, he turned his attention back to Collin. "I've risked my life for the people of this company more than once. That has to mean something."

Collin's gaze darted to the nearby tent before coming back to rest on Matt—still fierce, fury still mottling his cheeks red. He had to be wrestling with the fact that Matt had saved Stella's life at the risk of his own.

"There." Jason snipped off the thread with a quick flick of his wrist. He grabbed a roll of bandage from his bag. With deft fingers, his hands steady, he wrapped the material beneath Matt's arm and over his shoulder, his movements precise and economical.

Collin had moved away, now rubbing his face with his hand, speaking in low voices to Jordan.

"I've got to check on some of the others," Jason said to Collin. He rose, brushing dirt from his knees.

Matt scrambled to his feet, his boots slipping slightly as he pushed up. Lily knew this was the moment to make her escape. She took a faltering step backward, her pulse racing.

Her mind was sluggish, still whirling with this news, battered by Matt's betrayal.

"Lily, wait." His voice cracked.

She hadn't moved fast enough. He caught up with her in a couple of steps. When he reached out for her, she angled away so that her arm was out of reach. She tossed the shirt at him, the one she'd begged for from a neighbor. He caught it, wincing at the movement. His chest was still streaked with remnants of her sister's blood, an old scar across his midsection.

I only remember bits of my parents. The words he'd said to her only days ago. The stories of an impossible childhood skittered through her mind. She pressed her lips together as the memory surged.

Lies. Weren't they?

She didn't know what was true, what was a lie meant to gain her trust.

"Just give me a chance to explain," he said, voice low. He sent a look over his shoulder to Collin. He'd taken a step, as if he would come after Matt. Then Collin paused, his hand dropping to his side as he tilted his head, his gaze narrowing.

"What can there be to talk about?" Lily demanded. Her voice rose. "If it's true," she swallowed hard as she fought back tears, "if you truly work for those horrid men, there can be nothing left to say between us."

"Everything I told you was true," he said urgently. "I can barely remember my parents. I suffered on the streets, scrambling for food, eating scraps out of other people's refuse, nearly dying from the cold. The only thing I didn't tell you was that Amos Byrnes was the man who gave me a job when I was fifteen. He gave me a chance to escape those desperate straits." He searched her face.

She shook her head, closing her eyes. She didn't want to hear him speak good of the man he'd worked for. Byrnes ran illegal brothels and was cruel enough to have sent the men to kill them to get that ruby.

"If you work for him, you're just like him," she said, opening her eyes. Her lashes clumped together with the tears she refused to let fall.

Her words hit. She saw his flinch, the flicker of pain that crossed his face.

"I never hurt anybody," he said with resignation in his voice. "I moved crates and barrels and boxes in the shipping yards. Sometimes I lied to the inspectors and the toll collectors—sometimes I rushed a job so no one would find out my bosses were shipping things they weren't supposed to—but I never hurt or killed anyone to make my work happen."

She stifled a sob. "That doesn't matter. Working for him meant making money for him, so he could pay those men out there who are trying to kill us now."

"Lily, listen—" He leaned forward, his good hand reaching toward her again.

She spun away. "Maybe you think you've changed, but you're still the same man you were when you left New York City."

He went still, his face hardening into an unreadable mask, his eyes dark.

Her breath hitched, eyes burning with the flood of tears she wouldn't let fall.

He'd never truly been her friend, just someone playing a part. He admitted that he'd lied. She couldn't believe anything he said, not anymore.

"The children need me. Don't ever speak to me again." She whirled and walked away, keeping her shoulders straight so he wouldn't see the sobs already overtaking her.

Chapter Fifteen

MATT LAY beneath one of the wagons, wrapped in a blanket, his injured shoulder throbbing.

Night had fallen, but everything was quiet. Collin and the other men had relieved him of his weapons, had tethered his horse with the others. He wasn't bound hand and foot, like Byrnes's other man, but they'd made it abundantly clear that they were watching his every move, and if he did anything suspicious, he would be shot on sight.

His only saving grace was that he had tried to save Stella. Collin couldn't believe him all bad when it came to that.

Stella was still hanging on. They'd rigged the tent differently after Jason had taken a jagged piece of wood, one that had exploded off one of the wagons, out of another pioneer's hip. One side of the tent was closed, the other open. Maddie slept near that tent. He didn't know where Doc had gone off to.

He had held everything he wanted in his hands. Lily had

clung to him this afternoon, worried over him. *"I care about you,"* she had said.

Other memories wound through his mind. Lily's claim that Elsie would've liked him if she'd known him now. Watching her feed the calf, hold little Jenny. Tease the boys.

Holding Lily in his arms on the cliffside. On the back of his horse during the firefight.

Their first night together, huddled beneath his coat to stay warm in the snowfall. He'd been hovering on the edge of sleep, his mind fuzzy and slow. Even then, there'd been some part of him that wanted to have her closer. Wrap her in his arms and never let go.

He was a fool.

Right now it didn't matter that fire radiated from the wound in his shoulder or that they were in mortal danger. His brain had started spinning dreams of what a future with Lily might be like: settling a homestead in Oregon, raising her baby—

His mind cut off the thought there. What did he know about being a father? He'd never had one. It was only something else for him to fail at, a job he wasn't worthy to do.

But that didn't stop the ache that had overtaken his entire body.

He wanted that life with Lily. Wanted her light to shine brightly in his life every day. And he'd gone and ruined it all.

He felt as if he was breaking apart from the inside.

Collin and Jordan sat in the dark nearby, eating cold biscuits. "There has to be a way out," Jordan said.

"Too many stars out tonight," Collin said. "There's no cover along the valley floor."

"If we could get past those quicksand pits, the canyon walls aren't so sheer. We could climb up and come around behind them," Jordan said.

"But we can't swim through those quicksand pits." Collin shook his head. "If a man tried to cross them, he'd sink faster than a stone, and that would be the end of him."

Jordan muttered something too low to hear.

Matt's memory threw him back to when Lily had been trying to climb that hill with a twisted ankle, determination etched on her features. She'd suggested that a plank or a barrel lid might provide enough of a flat surface for a man to walk across the quicksand.

It couldn't be like walking in snowshoes, he thought, even as another part of him wondered if it would be worth a try.

It wasn't his fight, he reminded himself. The men had made that clear. They didn't want his help.

And Lily didn't want him.

Every one of her words had pounded him with the strength of a battering ram. She'd spoken the truth. He could've come clean at any time. He could've made other choices. Not worked for Amos at all or walked away the first time Amos asked him to skirt around the law. The reality was, he was scum from the streets. A man with no parents, no home, no legacy.

He'd seen Collin crumple earlier in the evening, worried over his wife. Watched Leo come alongside him and sling an arm around his brother's shoulder. They had a bond so strong it couldn't be broken, one that gave Collin support even in these darkest hours.

He'd heard whispers later. Hadn't known before today that Stella was carrying a baby, just like Lily. Would her unborn child survive the injury? Would Stella?

Matt had never had any kind of brotherly bond. Never experienced love as strong as the love Maddie showed in the hours she toiled over her sister, still not leaving her sister's side.

Even Alex and Paul—the way they doted on little Jenny, the way they argued but had such fierce loyalty toward each other.

He'd never been deserving of any of that. Never would be. He couldn't change who he was. *Eye for an eye.* That was from the Bible, though he couldn't remember whether Rusty had said the words or if he'd heard them somewhere else. He deserved whatever punishment was coming his way.

But there had to be a way to get Lily and the kids, and the other pioneers, out of here.

If he snuck out of camp, pretended he had the ruby in his possession, could he approach the sharpshooter? Now that his weapons had been confiscated, it would be nearly impossible to overpower the other hired gun out there.

His mind whirled, trying to think of any solution that meant safety for Lily and the others. It might be the only thing he had left to give her.

* * *

Lily jolted awake, chilly air stinging her face. Her knees were bent in front of her, her back resting against one of the wagon wheels.

With so many folks injured—and Coop and Rob separated from the wagons—Leo had asked every able-bodied person to stay on watch tonight. Irene still hadn't been found. And Lily knew Leo feared an outright attack.

She had a rifle across her lap, though she still wasn't entirely certain she could use it.

The night around her was quiet. What had woken her?

She felt as if she hadn't slept at all. Had she only just now dozed off? After one sleepless night and then the terror they'd been through earlier in the day, her body felt weighted down by exhaustion. But now that she was awake, her brain raced with thoughts.

She was such a dunce, falling for Matt when he was nothing more than a liar. Stella had warned her, had cautioned Lily against falling for the man who had portrayed himself as a hired hand. Had Stella seen what Lily hadn't? Had she somehow seen through Matt's façade?

Thinking about her sister only brought on the threat of more tears. The hot knot clogged her throat. Stella still hadn't woken. The last time Lily had spoken to Maddie, she had seen the worry her sister couldn't hide. Stella's injury was life-threatening. She'd lost so much blood.

Nothing stirred out in the darkness. But then a twig snapped, and Lily startled. Was that movement nearby?

Her heart hammered. Something was wrong. Her fingers tightened on the rifle's stock as dread coiled in her chest.

A shadow shifted around the side of the wagon, but before Lily could raise the weapon or clamber to her feet, a form stepped into the moonlight.

Irene. Hair tangled, eyes wild. She had one arm around Alex's shoulders, holding him almost like a shield in front of her body. In her other hand, she had what looked like a sharp rock. Its point looked jagged enough to cut through the tender flesh of his throat, where Irene held it in threat.

Lily's chest seized, breath going shallow.

"Quiet," Irene ordered. Her hand twitched on Alex's shoulder.

"Alex—" Lily's voice broke.

"I said quiet." Irene's eyes glinted wild in the moonlight, her jagged rock pressing harder against Alex's throat, a faint tremor in her arm.

Alex shook in her hold, eyes wide with panic. Irene pressed the rock deeper, a thin line of blood welling against his skin.

"Drop your gun. If you call out, I'll kill him right here." Irene's voice brooked no argument. Lily fumbled to set the rifle on the ground. It landed with a dull thud.

Now what? Her heart thundered as her gaze locked on Alex. She willed him to stay calm, silently pleading with him not to move.

How had Irene gotten to him? Had he been up in the night, needing the privy? Or had she somehow snuck into the children's wagon in the circle and wakened him violently from sleep?

"Stella, where's the ruby?" Irene was clearly out of it, mistaking Lily for her sister once again.

Stella was still unconscious—she might never wake up. Lily's breath hitched, her fingers scrabbling on the ground beside her for anything she might use. A rock? She couldn't raise the gun without risking Irene stabbing Alex.

"I know you've got it," Irene whispered. She glanced around frantically.

"I don't know," Lily said, forcing her voice to stay calm. Her eyes flickered to Alex. He was shaking.

Stella had never told her where she'd hidden the ruby even after all this time. Maybe Stella thought she was protecting her sisters, but at this moment, Lily wished nothing more than that she had the ruby to trade for Alex. How could she get him out of the madwoman's grasp?

The weight of it settled heavily on Lily. She was alone. There was no one for her to turn to for help. Not Stella, who was so gravely injured; not Maddie, tending to her sister; not Matt, who'd betrayed her and whom she'd told to stay away.

She was well and truly alone in an agonizing, dangerous situation. The grip of loneliness—desperation for someone to stand by her side, to help her—almost swallowed her whole. What could she do on her own? She had failed to keep Alex safe—she had no one to turn to.

But Irene didn't seem to care about her internal turmoil.

"I want the ruby. Now." Irene's rock pressed closer into Alex's throat. He flinched, mouth opening in a small gasp, the noise sharp in the quiet.

"I'm going to stand up." Lily pushed to her feet. "It's in

the wagon." She held both hands out to show that she was unarmed. "Let Alex go, and I'll get it for you."

"Ain't no way I'm letting him go until I have that jewel in my hand."

Dread pooled cold in Lily's gut. Irene wouldn't let Alex go.

"Get inside and get it," Irene's voice grated harsh.

She had no choice but to tiptoe to the Fairfax wagon. "It might take a second," Lily said. "You don't need to keep a hold of Alex."

"You think I'm a fool? The moment I let go of him, he's going to be shouting for help."

Lily scrambled into the wagon, looking for anything she might use to overpower Irene. A revolver, a knife. Outside the canvas, Irene's whisper came to her. "Find it, Stella. Now!"

Alex's small whimper stabbed Lily right in the heart. She ran her fingers over a crate—a barrel. Where would Stella have hidden the ruby? Her chest heaved as she attempted to calm her emotions. She was alone. She didn't know where the ruby was. She couldn't call out for help.

Fear clawed at her throat and sent silent tears spilling down her cheeks.

What was she going to do?

Chapter Sixteen

MATT REMAINED where he'd been put, though Collin and Jordan had moved off. The sky was brimming with stars, but he was keeping half an eye on Byrnes's man, who was still tied up but snoring softly now. Matt's shoulder throbbed in a steady beat along with his heart, and his breath clouded faintly in front of him as the night got colder. He still didn't have any answers. And he couldn't help wondering if Lily was all right somewhere in that circle of wagons. He hoped she was curled up asleep with the children, able to find some comfort and rest in this terrifying night.

He knew she would never forgive him. He couldn't ask for it, not given what he'd done.

The rustle of a blanket from nearby caused him to turn his head. There was movement in that half-tent that had been erected for those with the most seriously injured. Was it Stella moving?

He strained his eyes, trying to see through the dark.

"Water," a voice rasped low. Stella's voice.

A glance at Maddie said she was still lost to sleep—she probably needed it, given how much they'd all been through.

"Hang on," he whispered. He got up and crept to the tent, keeping a careful distance from her and the other injured pioneer, not daring to even touch her on the chance that he might make her injury worse. He drew the dipper from a bucket of clean water and gently brought it to her lips with his good hand.

She drank a few sips and then shook her head. Her gaze locked on his shoulder, pain lines etched around her eyes. Matt set the dipper down, but her hand caught his wrist, her grip stronger than he expected from a woman in her condition.

"I've been in and out all evening," she murmured. He glanced to see if her voice had woken Maddie, but the other sister slept on. "Is it true? Do you work for Byrnes?"

His throat tightened. He wished he could tell her something else, but it needed to be the truth. "That's how it started." He shook his head slightly, sitting back on his heels. "The truth is, I don't know who I am anymore."

He waited, squatted there in the darkness, breathing shallow, expecting her to flay him open, to call him the worthless fool that he was. Her gaze held steady, somehow piercing through the dark.

"I think you're the man who noticed how much my sister is hurting—you're the one who told me to make up with her." She shifted the slightest amount—her face crumpling in pain. Then she went still. "I almost didn't have a chance. Now I will, thanks to you."

Her affirmation struck the deepest part of him.

"I see the way you look at her when you think no one is looking," she rasped. "Like you're starving for a meal you'll never have."

Starved for Lily. That fit. He felt the same way he had at fifteen. Empty, wanting, desperate.

He turned his face away, heat rising in his cheeks despite the cold air's bite. He'd admitted why he'd saved Stella to Lily earlier. It would've killed her if her sister had passed. She needed Stella in her life. "I could never deserve her," he whispered.

Stella squeezed his wrist and then let go, her hand flopping down to her side as if just that much movement had exhausted her. "Scripture says it plain. Jesus didn't come for folks already righteous."

Rusty had been preaching the same thing at Matt for weeks.

She wasn't done. "He came to seek and save the lost." There was a thread of warmth in her voice, one that burrowed into a deep place inside of him.

Was it really as easy as Rusty had said, over and over? Matt didn't want to be the same man he had been when he left New York, but did God really want the likes of him?

The truth of Stella's soft statement—and everything that Rusty had told him over the past weeks—filtered through all of the broken pieces of Matt's heart, settling deep. He wanted the new life God promised. Wanted to follow Jesus, wanted to have his fractured heart healed. Even if he couldn't have Lily.

He bowed his head as the weight of his desire to be new settled over him, a quiet peace stealing through the storm within. A peace even in the midst of the uncertainty about what would happen to the wagon train, what might happen if they survived this and reunited with the company. Matt might be ejected from the wagon train, given that he'd joined up under false pretenses.

But in the light of this new revelation—this new truth settling deep inside Matt's heart—the danger and the uncertainty didn't matter.

"Thank you," he whispered.

Stella's eyes fluttered. Was she already drifting off again? It had to be a good sign that she'd woken to drink water.

Matt put the dipper and bucket away in the darkness, heart thundering. He took a steadying breath. He had a new life, a chance to be someone worthy. Not because of the things that Matt had done, but because of Jesus's sacrifice.

The stars that had seemed so distant and cold minutes ago now twinkled warmly at him. A new determination strengthened him. He wouldn't let this be the end.

* * *

Lily couldn't seem to raise her head from where it rested on her folded arms. She cried silent tears, panic engulfing her body, her mind spinning so that she could barely sense or feel her surroundings. Everything narrowed to the darkness behind her eyes, the next breath.

When her chest grew so tight she feared she couldn't inhale at all, she felt a quiet whisper that sounded like an echo of her sister's voice: "Just take the next breath."

She could hear Irene mumbling, though her mind was so unfocused that she couldn't make out the words. It sounded as if Irene had rounded the wagon to the outside of the circle; she'd be more hidden on that side, but it was also only a few feet away from the quicksand pits, making it dangerous.

Alex.

Alex needed her.

But Lily was frozen in panic and indecision.

Irene's voice rasped, her words audible and frantic this time. "I've been on my own—starving—claiming back what's mine."

On my own.

The words were an echo of Lily's desperation.

"Hurry up, girl."

Lily's fingers fumbled over a crate's rough edge, searching without seeing in the gloom inside the wagon.

"I am with you always." The scripture Maddie had shared days ago flooded into Lily's mind.

All of a sudden, she had a vivid memory of Stella sitting cross-legged on the bed. She'd been much younger, reading from the family Bible with halting words—probably been barely old enough to read them. That wasn't the only time Stella, and later Maddie, had shared a nightly ritual and read the Bible aloud before they all retired for the night. Those readings had given Lily a foundation of faith.

She'd had so much trouble lately clinging to that faith after suffering so much loss. But the more she remembered, the more peace she began to feel.

After Ma had died, the three sisters had been left with an absentee father, one who rarely cared whether they were in the apartment with him or not. Stella and Maddie had done everything they could to make sure that Lily had the happiest childhood possible. They'd given up their own food, given up what few enjoyments they might've had. After their father passed away, Stella became the provider for the three of them, and she'd never once complained. They'd eaten late suppers together after Stella came home from a long and grueling workday. They were a family, tied with a bond of loyalty that was unbreakable.

She couldn't understand—maybe would never understand—why Harry's life had been cut short. It could just as easily have been Lily struck by that snake. He hadn't even known about the baby she carried, that he would've been a father. Had it been one last instinct—protecting Lily—that had cost his life?

Yet even in those moments, God had been with her. God had brought her sisters to her side. Maddie had promised not to abandon her, and even though they'd faced difficult times lately, Lily knew how very deeply Stella loved her, even if she was too stubborn to say the words.

God had been faithful through all of it. Lily clung to that truth, let it settle over her like a shawl, bringing warmth and new life to her limbs, all the way down to her fingertips. She leaned on the faith developed at her sisters' knees from such a young age. She'd forgotten, put it aside, and let the worries and fears of being on this journey overtake her.

But no longer. Maybe she didn't have help in this moment, but she wasn't alone. New strength filled her. What could she use to get herself and Alex out of this situation? She felt around her, fingers closing over the handle of the heavy cook pot. She could try to bludgeon Irene, but what if Alex got in the way? What if he was injured?

Irene was murmuring now. It was clear her patience was wearing thin.

Lily's fingers brushed a smooth object, tucked in a bowl with several others. An egg. It was cool, and the shell firm when she raised it in her palm. Her pulse leaped with a spark of an idea. This egg was about the same size as the ruby.

She grabbed a handkerchief from her pocket and gently wrapped the egg inside it.

She sent out a prayer for strength, and her hands were steady as she found her way to the back of the wagon. "I'm coming," she called out softly.

She disembarked with the cloth-wrapped egg tucked in her hand. Irene was rocking back and forth now, Alex was still clutched in her arm, that rock still threatening at his throat. He was pale, his eyes even wider than they'd been before.

Hang on, she urged him silently with her eyes. *This is almost over.*

Lily held out the cloth-wrapped egg. "Here."

Before Irene could move, Lily tossed it away from the wagon.

For a split second, Irene's arm loosened from around Alex. She lunged toward where the egg had bounced into the darkness along the ground.

Lily grabbed for Alex. "Help!" she cried out, even as she pushed him away. Irene was on all fours, scrambling for the egg. "Run, Alex! Get help!"

She heard him shout but didn't have time to watch his progress. She had to whirl and face Irene. The woman's face was pale, her eyes wild in the darkness.

"You lied!" She lifted up the handkerchief, now dripping with egg yolk and swung her other arm. Lily saw a flash of that rock in the moonlight. She twisted and then rammed her shoulder into Irene.

Irene was slight and fell to her knees. Though she scrambled to her feet quickly, coming for Lily again. "I want my ruby. It's mine! He promised it to me. We were supposed to be married—"

She lunged for Lily again, but this time Alex darted from beneath the wagon.

He shoved Irene, but her bony hand gripped his wrist. Lily lunged for them, putting herself between them, but she couldn't pry Irene's grip from Alex.

"Maybe I'll go for the little girl next!"

"No!" Alex shouted.

Irene still wouldn't let go. Suddenly light shone through the break between the wagons. Someone had brought a torch.

Irene let go of Alex and shrank back angrily. She started to run—in the wrong direction.

"No!" Lily called out.

But it was too late. Irene stepped at the edge of the quicksand, stumbled, lost her balance, and fell into the sludge. Lily took two steps in that direction, but Alex grabbed her arm, pulling her back. When she glanced at him, he was wide-eyed and terrified, unable to tear his gaze away from Irene.

Lily remembered how quickly the sludge had covered Mr. Simmons's milk cow. She took a step away from the quicksand and pulled Alex to her, turning his head so he wouldn't see the woman's last moments.

Leo came running out from between the wagons, quickly followed by Jordan. The sound of Irene thrashing drew their attention before Leo could ask what was going on. And then a great, gaping gurgle sound. Followed by quiet. Lily bent her head close to Alex, trying to calm her breathing, trying to forget what she had just witnessed.

"Was that—" Leo started.

Lily nodded.

Alex backed away from her and blurted out, "She woke me up—held this sharp rock to my neck. I thought she was gonna stab me."

The boy told the two men everything. Jordan stalked to

the edge of the quicksand as if he wanted to make sure she wasn't going to rise up from its wet depths.

Leo caught Lily's elbow. "You all right?"

She nodded, still too upset to formulate words. She'd never wanted Irene to sink to her death. The woman had needed help. She'd been confused, upset, half-starved.

"Anything I can do for you?"

Lily shook her head. "I've got to get Alex calmed down and back in bed." She paused. "Is Matt... all right?"

A flash of surprise crossed Leo's face. He shrugged, eyes hardening. "Not sure you'd want to trust that two-timing snake."

After she assured him again she was all right, he strode away, leaving Jordan to keep watch on that side of the circled wagons.

Lily felt a pang of sadness for Matt, thinking of the boy who had been lost and alone on the streets of New York City. She had been frightened enough when her and her sisters' belongings had been stolen and they'd had nowhere to go. But they'd been adults. He'd only been a child when he'd faced such difficulty.

She didn't know whether she could trust him again— Leo was right about that—but she did know that she could forgive him. Imagining Alex being in the same position settled it in her mind, in her heart. Still, she didn't know what she would say if she saw Matt again.

That was a problem for another day.

Alex crawled into his bedroll beside Paul. "Shame she cared so much about that ruby."

Lily brushed a kiss on his forehead and moved outside the wagon. She was still too shaken to go back to sleep, but her new peace remained.

Ruby.

An idea lodged in Lily's mind. One she couldn't shake.

All this chaos, danger, death for a piece of jewelry. She knew she had to try and make things right.

Chapter Seventeen

DAWN WOULD COME SOON, but now it was still dark and quiet. The stars had faded to faint specks above, their light slowly growing dim against the black sky.

Most of the company was on watch, but back here, near the quicksand pits, it was quiet.

There'd been some kind of dust-up earlier in the night, but everything had settled again. Now Matt worked silently and by feel as he used a hammer to tap a nail, the soft clink echoing through the stillness. His breath clouded, rising in faint wisps.

Pain throbbed steadily in his left shoulder, the stitches Doc had put in still thrumming hot. Leo and Collin expected an attack from the front of the caravan, facing the valley's entrance. Matt had figured out a way he could help. Back here, where there was no one to interrupt him.

He couldn't sleep anyway. And no one had seen him moving around camp. He took that as a sign to keep going.

He grimaced, keeping his jaw clenched tight against the ache in his arm as he sliced another leather strap from an old harness and then nailed it carefully onto the second barrel lid lying on the ground at his feet.

It was almost done now. He hadn't dared to take a long look at the quicksand yet. The remembered danger of what he'd seen before made him breathless just thinking about it. Lily's idea was going to work. It had to.

"What are you doing?" A voice in the dark.

Collin.

Matt wouldn't show that he'd been startled. He put the last nail against the leather as Collin came to stand over him, a blur of darker shadow.

"How's Stella?" Matt whispered, hoping the other man would just go away.

No luck. "Sleeping. What are you doing?" Collin repeated.

"Lily had this idea a while back. To use barrel lids fashioned sort of like a snowshoe. She figured something flat and wide might let a man cross the quicksand without sinking." His left hand slipped, and white-hot agony pulsed through his shoulder. He gritted his teeth. "The way I figure it, if I can make it over to that edge—" he pointed with his good arm—"I can climb up and circle around."

"You take a weapon?"

That was a sticking point. "Not yet."

"Do you think you can climb with that bad arm?"

"I aim to."

Collin squatted next to Matt, his fingers touching the

edge of one of the barrel lids. When he spoke, it was with a quiet seriousness to his voice. "Irene sank into one of these pits earlier tonight. Only took a few seconds. Are you sure you wanna try?"

Matt didn't look at the other man. "I made a promise." Lily's expression of hurt and betrayal flashed through his mind. He'd shattered her trust. He wouldn't ask her to forgive him—how could she? But he could do this. "I won't let those sharpshooters get through to hurt Lily—or those kids."

It must've been the right thing to say, because Collin extended his hand, a revolver in his outstretched fingers.

"I figure we'll have to get close—stay out of their sights."

We?

"You know where I can find some more of those lids?"

Matt's throat tightened, hope flickering fragile. "You should stay. You've got to live for Stella, and..." The baby she was carrying. "Your brother and sister."

"Seems like you've got someone to live for, too," Collin said calmly.

A quiet ache bloomed as Matt shook his head. "Not anymore."

"Don't give up on her," Collin said. "She loves you."

He wanted to believe it—so much that the thought of it made his breath stick in his chest. But he couldn't quite believe it possible.

"You saved my wife. I can't let you go out there alone, not when you matter to Lily. You're family."

The words hit hard—Collin's explanation of what family did. That he was family.

A sense of belonging slipped over Matt like a warm coat, a bond forged in their shared purpose. Collin wanted to protect the women and children, too.

"There are more barrels in that near wagon."

Several minutes later, the two men stood at the quicksand's edge. Dawn would come soon. Their time was short, and they had a long way to travel on foot.

Both had their boots attached to the barrel lids with straps of leather.

Matt's heart sat in his throat. "Here we go," he breathed.

Matt prayed a silent prayer: *Lord, let this hold.*

He took the first step—slow, deliberate—letting the lid settle soft against the quicksand's surface. It wobbled, but he didn't sink—not even when he moved his second foot, slowly, and then his entire weight was on the surface.

It worked.

He spoke to Collin over his shoulder, "Move slowly. We can make it."

Only thirty more steps to go.

Collin followed Matt at a snail's pace. The farther they got toward the center of the pit, the more Matt's nerves strangled. If he miscalculated his balance, death waited.

Urgency pushed them toward the far edge. If the sun came up, it would be harder to hide from the men hunting them. They had to move quickly, but they couldn't afford any mistakes.

Matt reached solid ground first, Collin right behind him.

They slipped the barrel lids from their boots, both breathing hard.

"Let's go," Collin said fiercely.

Collin outpaced Matt as they climbed the steep, rocky hillside. Every step, every movement sent fire through Matt's shoulder. Yet there was no time for delay. He felt every scrape against his palm, every bruised knee, but he kept moving. He had to protect those he'd come to love.

The first tint of dawn rose as they crested the last hill. Collin knelt at the edge, peering down into the mouth of the valley. "Seems like shots were coming from there—" He pointed to a ridge a hundred yards away. "And there." Now he pointed to another one almost straight down the hillside.

"I'll go down." Matt was determined to find the shooter before the sun finished coming up.

They separated, Collin moving fast through the last of the darkness.

As light spread, every step made Matt feel exposed. He could only pray the shooter wasn't looking in this direction.

Movement in the distance caught his eye. Collin ambushed a man wearing a dark hat. One punch and the man hit the ground. Collin dragged the man behind a rock outcropping.

Hopefully, he would use the rope he'd carried with him to secure the man.

One down.

Matt's heart raced as he strained his eyes in the growing light. Where was Byrnes's other man?

There.

A patch of white, stark against the rust-colored rocks, twenty yards straight down. Matt edged to the side for a better view. The man lay on his belly, his rifle aimed toward the meadow.

Matt crept down the hill. His boots slipped. A few pieces of gravel rolled two feet before they stopped. He held his breath as he pulled the revolver from his belt. Had he been heard? It would be a tough shot at this distance.

The sky was lightening rapidly. He had to go now.

But the man hadn't moved. What was he watching with such careful attention?

Matt squinted to see the valley floor. A rider coming on a black horse.

His breath froze in his chest, then caved in. Lily, riding at a gallop, one arm raised.

What—? There was a sparkle of red—

Then he saw the flash of sun on the gun barrel, aimed right at her. Fear flooded him, but Matt moved fast—not caring now that rocks cascaded beneath his feet. The shooter looked up, then back to sighting the rifle. Had he judged Matt to be too far away?

An image of Stella—that spray of blood, her fall from the horse—flashed through Matt's mind.

No!

He was still too far from the shooter, so he jumped, landed hard against a boulder. Pain speared through his shoulder, so much that he nearly blacked out.

From a far distance, he heard her voice: "Matt!"

Lily.

The sharpshooter.

He rolled to throw himself off the last ledge with a roar. He felt the impact as he landed on top of the shooter. The gun went off. The clap of the weapon firing rocked in his ears and chest.

No!

A whinny.

The man rolled beneath Matt, but Matt managed to get both hands on the barrel of the gun. He gave one great shove with all his might, enough to yank the weapon from the man, even though flames seemed to lick his shoulder. He used the stock of the rifle on the man's head. His eyes rolled back, and he went still.

A woman's shout was followed by an answering one from Collin. Matt forced himself to his feet, even though his entire body felt weak from fear and grief. A groan. Not his. He looked down and knocked the man fully unconscious with the rifle.

He whirled. The black stallion stood on the valley floor, riderless. Had Lily been hit?

Collin was picking his way down the hillside, running in Matt's direction.

Matt took one step. The stallion took two steps forward, and then Matt spied Lily standing—no, running—toward him with tears on her face. She was alive.

Joy burst inside him. He took off, moving as quickly as he could, every step down that hill jarring his injured shoulder and providing him a new collection of bruises.

Lily met him at the foot of the hill. Her face was so dear,

tears streaming down her cheeks, that he couldn't help himself. He swept her into his arms.

Collin shouted. Matt turned his head. Movement. The sharpshooter was standing, raising his rifle.

Matt turned his back to the man, protecting Lily the only way he knew how. With his body.

A shot reverberated.

Matt flinched, but there was no bite of pain. He whipped his head around to see the man fall, wisps of smoke rising from Collin's rifle barrel.

Lily gasped. Matt turned his shoulder so she wouldn't have to see.

It was over.

Grateful tears stung his eyes. Lily was safe in his arms. He knew that the fact that her face was turned into his shoulder and she was shaking with sobs didn't mean she forgave him or returned his feelings. Her fierce trembling must mean she was as grateful as he that they'd survived. Even so, he couldn't quite force himself to let her go. He buried his nose in her hair, breathed in her scent. He couldn't feel his pain anymore. Only her. He would let himself take this one moment, especially if it was all he would have.

Lily leaned into Matt's strength, his good hand pressed warm against her back, and let his presence anchor her until her quaking stopped. She was aware of Collin moving closer. Was he checking that the shooter was really dead?

The crack of the rifle blast still echoed in her ears. Only remembering that Matt was hurt made her push back gently. Tears misted his eyes.

"Are you hurt?" Her gaze caught on the blood blooming through his shoulder—maybe more than yesterday. "You are."

She didn't wait for his answer, just leaned down to rip a length from her petticoat. She had nothing else out here to make a bandage with. When she pressed it to his shoulder, he winced faintly, and his hand closed over hers.

"I'm all right, Lily. I might've torn through the stitches, but I'll live."

"What do you think you're doing out here?" Collin's voice reminded her that they weren't alone.

Matt's gaze turned intent. "I'd like to know that, too."

She reached into her skirt pocket and pulled out the ruby. Holding it by the chain, she raised it and let it dangle between them. She'd stashed it in her pocket as she'd jumped from the horse when she saw Matt fling himself off the hill-side. Now it hung in the air, sparkling in the first rays of sunlight. "It's pretty, but I can't believe it caused so much trouble. I couldn't let that sharpshooter hurt the people I love."

There was a beat of silence between them, then Matt spoke, voice rough. "What are you gonna do with it?"

She realized she was still holding onto him and gently disentangled her hand to let it drop at her side. She couldn't quite look at him. "Do you need to take it back to New York City?"

He ducked his head. "I'm not going back." He swallowed hard, spoke again before she could respond. "I'm sorry for all of it, Lily. The lying, sneaking around, most of all for hurting you. I can't ask for your forgiveness, but you should know that meeting you has changed me. I want to start a new life. One I can be proud of."

Her heart thudded hard in her chest. There was so much she wanted to say to him, but when he looked at her again all she could find was, "What are you doing out here? He could've killed you."

His gaze met hers, his eyes dark. "I couldn't let him hurt you—not when I feel the way I do." Her heart flew, even with her awareness of Collin nearby. Was he scouting for more danger? She was too focused on Matt to look away and find out.

She slipped the ruby back in her pocket and took a tiny step toward Matt. "You said you couldn't ask my forgiveness, but you don't have to. You already have it."

His brows creased as if he didn't understand.

"Last night, Irene grabbed Alex—threatened him, demanded the ruby." Her voice caught in the remembered terror. "I realized I would do anything to keep him alive. How can I fault you for doing what it took for you to stay alive? When it counted—now—you've made the right choice."

His throat worked while a tentative hope lightened his eyes.

"Why don't you kiss her already?" Collin called out.

Matt glanced away, a muscle jumping in his cheek. When he looked back at her, she saw the war with himself in his eyes.

She stepped forward, reached for him, tipped her head.

His kiss was tentative, searching. When his arm came around her, she drew back for breath, to press the makeshift bandage against his shoulder again before losing herself in his kiss. His arm came around her.

It felt like a homecoming—like the promise of a new future, warm and certain amid the light of a new day.

"Men on horseback coming from camp!" Collin called out.

Matt drew back, but she didn't let go of him. She kept pressure on his wound. She needed to touch him. There was so much emotion spilling out of his gaze.

"I'm falling in love with you," he said, his voice deep and gravelly.

Distant shouts rose faint, but she couldn't look away as joy bubbled up within her.

"I'm falling in love with you, too."

She saw the surprise and then relief pass through his eyes. Hadn't he guessed? Now she was certain tears stood in his eyes before he closed them and let his forehead rest against hers.

She let herself revel in this closeness, in each steady breath that he took, with beats that drew them closer.

Leo called out, Collin answering, though she couldn't make out the words. She wouldn't move away from the protective embrace of the man God had used to help rescue her and her family. And to rescue her heart. She would always care for Harry. She still grieved what might've been, that her baby would never know his or her father. But God had poured out blessings by putting Matt in her life. She would never take that for granted.

Chapter Eighteen

EVENING WAS FALLING, a long day behind the pioneers. Lily was breathing slowly through the nausea until it passed. This time, no panic followed on its heels.

Slowly, methodically, she worked at putting the tent up for the night.

Blossom bleated as she romped with Paul and Alex and Ben nearby. Milk had been difficult to come by, but she knew she would figure something out. She smiled a little as she watched the calf and the children playing. It was good to see the children happy. They had spent a couple of fearful days after the attack on their company. It helped when they caught up with the rest of the company, led by Hollis, two days after that final altercation. Maddie and Jason had spent a busy few days doctoring the pioneers who'd needed help. It was only Stella who remained under their care now.

Matt rode along the edge of camp and doffed his hat to her—he was probably heading to the cowboy camp to help with supper. He truly intended to make a new start, so he'd kept to his deal with Leo and Collin. He'd need the cash he'd earned by pushing those cattle when they got to Oregon.

She knew he would come by for a walk later—he'd come every night, and most mornings. They usually walked and talked for hours. Then Lily would take her turn to sit with Stella through the night. Her sister's fever had come on as they'd left the valley. They'd made a bed for Stella in the family wagon. Collin rarely left her side, though he did need to catch some sleep during the night. Maddie needed a break as well. Taking the night shift allowed Lily to be with her sister without having to face her yet. There was still so much unsaid between them.

Lily finished tying off the canvas and stepped back to admire her handiwork. She'd done it. Pitched the tent all on her own. And it was rock-solid. She'd been borrowing books on homesteading from Evangeline and had begun slowly compiling a plan for what she might do once they all reached the Willamette Valley.

She was still smiling when Maddie called out to her. Things were settled now in the company. There were only the dangers of the trail in the wilderness, no more men chasing them, but it didn't stop Lily's heart from pounding when she heard her name. She had to tell herself that everything was all right.

The one man Collin had caught and tied up had been brought back to the company, but before Hollis could decide on and mete out his punishment, he had broken free of his bonds, tried to run away, and met an untimely end scrambling down a cliffside.

Lily didn't want to think about that.

Maddie motioned to the wagon, calling out, "Stella's awake! She wants you."

Maddie squeezed Lily's shoulder as she walked away from the wagon. Lily held her breath as she climbed gingerly inside. Stella lay still—her face pale, hair loose around her shoulders. A single candle sat on a plate in one corner, throwing flickering light. The air held a faint tang of medicinal herbs, sharp against the musty canvas. Stella's eyes were open, her expression unreadable. But she was alive. A powerful feeling of gratitude swelled fierce inside Lily. She knelt at her sister's side, her skirts rustling softly against the wagon's wooden floor.

"How can I help you? What can I do?" Lily's hands hovered over Stella's blanket, not sure whether she could touch her sister without causing hurt.

Stella grasped Lily's fingers in a surprisingly strong grip. "Forgive me." Stella's expression softened, her eyes glistening in the candlelight.

Sudden tears pricked Lily's eyes.

"I'm sorry," Stella whispered, her voice barely audible as she shifted slightly, wincing, "for trying to control everything, for putting you and Maddie—everyone—in danger."

Lily put her other hand over her sister's. Her fingers tightened, anchoring them both. "We're all safe now."

"Thanks to you." Stella's brows drew together. She exhaled, a soft rasp, her chest rising slightly under the blanket. She took a breath. "It's strange. Sometimes when I look at you, I see the little Lily who needed me to plait her hair, who snuggled into my lap for a cuddle at night." She exhaled softly as Lily sniffled. "But you are right. You're all grown up. I'm sorry for—"

"I'm sorry for pushing you away," Lily blurted, her voice cracking as she leaned closer, her knees pressing into the hard floor. "For keeping secrets—and for the things I said. You're my big sister, and I love you."

"I love you, too." Stella shook their connected hands, her grip faltering briefly before tightening again. "I heard what your cowboy did to take out those two sharpshooters."

Pride expanded Lily's heart. She straightened slightly, her shoulders easing as a small smile tugged at her lips. Everyone in the company had heard what Matt did, thanks to Collin. Matt quickly credited their idea for crossing the quicksand to her. She took a steadying breath. "He is my cowboy," she admitted. "I care about him a great deal, and I think you'll like him, too, once you get to know him."

Stella's eyes were warm. She tilted her head, a faint crease forming on her brow as she studied Lily. "He came to talk to me yesterday, even rode alongside the wagon for a bit."

Lily hadn't known. Her breath caught.

"He asked whether he could court you." Stella's voice softened in a rarely-shown tenderness.

Lily's heart leapt.

"I told him you make your own choices." Stella's hand squeezed hers.

Lily let the words, and her sister's confidence in her,

settle deep. She exhaled, the tension in her chest loosening, as the candle's flicker cast soft shadows across the canvas walls. She'd longed for this reparation of the relationship between them.

"What will we do with the ruby?" Lily asked.

"I told Collin to give it to Hollis. That jewel has caused so much trouble for our family. We'll find a future in Oregon without it." Stella's jaw tightened.

Lily nodded. Her gaze dropped to their joined hands, the candlelight glinting off her sister's ring. If she had her way, she would never see that stone again. She swallowed, knowing that she had more to say to her sister. "I was wrong before, too. Family matters. After God, it's the most important thing. I wanna make my homestead close to yours—you and Maddie—so our children can grow up knowing their cousins."

A tear slipped down Stella's cheek. Her hand trembled in Lily's, her breath hitching. "I might not—the baby—" She took a shaky breath.

"What did Doc say about your baby?" Lily's stomach knotted. Her fingers tightened around Stella's.

"That the human body is a wondrous thing, but the trauma might cause a miscarriage." Stella sniffled, a rare show of emotion from her strong sister. "We won't know— we have to wait and see."

Lily bent to press her forehead against their connected hands. Her tears fell silently, dampening the blanket, the wagon's faint creak underscoring her silent prayer. There were no words, only a heartfelt plea that God would save her sister's baby. When she raised her head, Stella whispered, "You'll be a wonderful mother, Lily."

"I learned how from you and Maddie," Lily responded.

Stella moved gingerly, wiping away the tears falling down her cheeks. "Look at us. Two watering pots. We need something else to talk about. Will you wear your special dress when you marry?"

"No." Lily's voice was steady, calm. "I have another idea for it."

She'd wanted a way to show Matt exactly what he meant to her, and an idea had come to her just now. They hadn't spoken of the future. She could feel him holding back sometimes. And Lily hadn't brought it up. She'd wanted to wait until Stella had recovered.

Now that her sister's fever had broken, Lily felt a new confidence. Stella would recover. There was still a long road ahead, possibly more grief waiting, but Lily would be by her side the whole time.

"I need more of a distraction," Stella said with a slight moan. "I'm cooped up with no end in sight. Tell me about your calf."

Lily smiled, grateful for her sister, for the family that God had restored to her.

* * *

Camp was quieting down, folks taking to their beds or getting ready to. Matt felt loud and conspicuous as he led a black milk cow around the edge of camp toward the Fairfax tents and wagon. An older man crouched over his fire tipped his hat at Matt, who nodded awkwardly. It turned out going after the two killers with Collin had made him into some kind of hero in the company's eyes. He didn't quite know what to do with the attention.

He'd had a long talk with Leo and Collin, and they'd agreed to let him stay on as a hired hand. Once they reached Oregon, Matt would be paid. Not much, but it was a start. He'd also had a long talk with Rusty after which he'd given his heart completely to Jesus, had his sins washed away in an icy mountain stream. He still couldn't describe the feeling of utter freedom at knowing he was forgiven.

Tonight, he wanted to do something to show Lily how much he loved her. And maybe his gift would ease her mind about one aspect of the future. His shoulder gave a tiny throb beneath the sling he wore to keep his arm still. He'd healed up a lot in the days since they'd left that terrifying canyon behind. It rarely ached with the fierceness it had before. He figured that meant it was healing.

His boots halted near Lily's family rig, and he took a moment to ground-tie the cow behind the conveyance so she wouldn't see it. Not yet. He brushed off his hands on his pants, straightened his hat, and walked into the circle of camp.

He found her by the fire with Jenny on her lap, while Maddie and the boys finished their cleanup. Her face brightened the moment she saw him.

Alex and Paul called out, their voices overlapping. "We

wanna hear it again." "Yeah, tell us about how you and Collin crossed that quicksand."

He laughed even as Lily chastised them, "You've heard that story six times already."

"Matt is brave for certain," Lily said. "But he doesn't need to tell it again tonight."

Suddenly bashful, he cleared his throat. "Do you reckon you'd walk with me a bit?"

"Of course." Lily stood with a rustle of skirts and handed the baby to Maddie. With the boys' chatter in the background and Maddie's smile encouraging them, Lily came to him, tugging her shawl close around her shoulders. She tucked her arm through the crook of his good elbow. He gazed down at her, couldn't quite get his feet moving.

"You're so beautiful," he murmured. "Someday I'd like to see you in that fancy dress I've heard about."

Her eyes widened for a moment, and she frowned slightly. "Actually, I don't have it anymore."

He shrugged. "No matter. I can't imagine you more beautiful than you are right now."

She flushed, and he finally got his feet moving.

They'd only gone a few steps when she caught sight of the cow and stopped short.

"Who's this?" she asked, a half-laugh in her voice.

"Farmer told me her name's Daisy." It seemed appropriate, since Lily had named her calf Blossom.

"What's she doing here?" Her voice held with innocent curiosity.

"She's a gift. For you. She'll give enough milk for Blossom and the kids until we get to Oregon."

"Oh, Matt." Her voice fell into a whisper.

His chest swelled, her appreciation spreading through him warmly.

She stepped over to the cow and scratched the docile animal's head.

"How—?" She shook her head. "Never mind. I have a gift for you, too." She turned toward him, fishing something out of her dress pocket. His heart thrummed in his ears.

"Nobody's ever given me a gift before. At least not one that didn't have strings attached."

Her expression softened as she opened her hands to reveal a beautiful brass pocket watch.

His chest tightened. "Lily—"

He shook his head, couldn't find words. "You shouldn't have. It's too much."

She was the only one who could've known what it meant to him. She pressed the watch into his palm, a weight that set his heart pounding.

"I was trying to wait until I had some money saved, some security, but—" the breath rushed out of him as she watched him with wide eyes. "But I don't want to spend one more day without you. I love you so much. I know it'll be a while before I can provide for us properly, but I want to marry you."

"Yes." Her quiet, firm answer raised his eyes to meet hers. "I'll marry you. I love you, too."

Joy crashed over him. He drew her close with his one

good arm, her gift clutched carefully in his palm. He kissed her with all the overflowing emotion inside him.

She pulled back breathlessly moments later. "I want to see it on your chain."

There was a beat of quiet before he spoke. "I don't have it anymore. I—I traded it." He motioned to the cow with a wry chuckle.

She blinked and then smiled with a shake of her head. "I traded my dress for your watch. I wanted you to have it."

She'd given up her fancy dress to give him his dream; he'd traded away the gold chain for her future. The knowledge settled deep as she nestled into the curve of his arm, looking at the cow and the silhouetted mountains beyond, a quiet certainty of love binding them together. He'd never imagined experiencing a love this deep and all-encompassing, never dreamed God would give him a future like the one that stretched out in front of him. He didn't need a fancy house, didn't need a bureau full of fine suits. All he needed was Lily. She was his heart—and his home.

Epilogue

FROST CRUNCHED beneath Coop's boots, the midmorning air laced with pine. Rob walked several yards ahead on the narrow deer path along a hillside. Every so often, dangerous drop-offs reminded Coop that he needed to be fully alert. He held the reins of the horse with Belle riding on its back through the quiet canyon woods.

Too quiet?

He tried to widen his awareness. He and Rob had walked—with Belle riding—through the entire day yesterday, through most of the night, and started again this morning. His legs felt heavy, his stomach growled. He flexed cold hands in his gloves. Coop was attuned to every noise, every rustle of every leaf. He didn't like being separated from the company, from the protection of his brothers. But it was more than that.

He glanced over his shoulder at Belle, whose eyes scanned the woods. She was always silent. He'd tried to engage her in conversation yesterday, plying her with questions—Where are you from? Who's your family? She'd ignored every one. He'd stopped after he'd caught Rob's smirk.

Now Coop moved back to walk beside the horse, opening the saddlebag to pull out a strip of jerky. He offered it to Belle. "Here. It's tough, but it might fill you up."

She hesitated, then grabbed it from his fingers without touching him. Questions filled his mind again. What had happened to her? Where had she escaped from? Why was she so afraid? He caught Rob's over-the-shoulder glance, the man's eyes flicking to Belle and back to Coop with a scowl. Coop narrowed his eyes. If he had more supplies, he would've shared—maybe.

Rob stopped and turned, hands on his hips. "This place looks awful familiar." His voice was laced with suspicion.

Coop shook his head. He didn't owe the other man an answer.

Rob refused to be brushed off. He pointed at a narrow pine, a recognizable landmark. "I've seen that tree before, when you were leading us at daybreak. Did we walk in a circle?"

The demanding tone set Coop off, his patience frayed. Even if Rob was right and that tree was a sure fire landmark.

"We've been out in these wilds for months," he said easily. "You're just imagining it."

Rob's eyes sparked fire, and Coop's temper longed to

return to the tussle that Alice had interrupted days ago. Rob took a step toward him. Coop met him, moving as far as the reins would allow him to go without dropping them.

He lowered his voice. "I think somebody might be tracking us."

There was a soft gasp. Coop looked back over his shoulder to see Belle's eyes fixed on him, her mouth trembling. If possible, her face had gone paler.

"I didn't want to say anything," he said. "It might be nothing. Just this feeling I got."

He wished he'd talked with August more. August would've told him what to look for, how to stay a step ahead if someone really was tracking the three of them out here.

"Maddie told me that somebody might be after Belle."

"Why didn't she tell anyone else?" Rob exploded. "If this slip of a girl is putting us in danger, that seems like something the company should be aware of!"

"He doesn't want anyone but me." Belle's voice, musical and soft, drew both Coop's and Rob's attention. She was visibly shaking, whether from Rob's outburst or the thought that someone was following them, Coop didn't know. She'd taken her knife from her pocket—or wherever she usually kept it. It quivered in her hand, resting on her thigh.

"I'm not gonna let anybody hurt you," Coop said.

"You can't promise that," Rob argued. "If he's a sharpshooter like the others back there, you could be in his sights right now."

A soft sob escaped her, and Coop lost the fragile hold on his temper. He shoved Rob. "Shut up! Don't scare her."

The horse whinnied, pulling on the reins, and for a moment, Coop thought that maybe Belle had leaned into the saddle, trying to break away from the men and escape, though it would be foolish for her to set out on her own out here.

As he whirled, he caught motion in his peripheral vision. A horse up on the ridge. A reddish bay that wasn't camouflaged by the trees and brush.

He started to tell Rob that he was going to get on that horse with Belle and ride away, but before he could say anything, a gunshot rang out, loud and close.

He must've moved at just the right moment, because a brush of air and the slightest whistle of pain grazed his upper arm.

"Get down!" he shouted to Rob, who had jumped away. Coop drew his revolver, swinging to try and sight where that shot had come from.

There. A log lying on the ground, a dozen yards up the hillside. The outline of a man's hat. Coop fired in that direction.

His horse reared. Belle slipped from the saddle and landed on the ground with a thud that threw Coop's heart into his throat. He dropped the reins and dove for her, trying to shield her with his body.

Another shot. Dust and dirt flew up from a foot in front of him. Coop fired again.

Where had Rob gone?

He glanced into Belle's terrified face. She hadn't made a sound, possibly so afraid that she'd frozen completely. They couldn't stay out here in the open. He snaked one arm around her waist and rolled to his feet, firing again, hoping to keep that shooter tucked behind his log.

Coop herded Belle up and over the next part of the trail which held no big trees to hide behind, only narrow aspens that didn't provide any cover. Somewhere below, the sound of rushing water grew louder.

Someone crashed through the woods behind him. The shooter was taking no pains to hide himself. Apparently, he just wanted Rob and Coop out of the way.

Coop pushed Belle forward, told her to keep running and not look back. He turned, raised his revolver, ready to take aim, only to find himself facing a man who was already in a stance, a handful of yards away, finger on the trigger.

All of a sudden, Rob threw himself out from behind a boulder that Coop hadn't paid one whit of attention to. Rob landed on the shooter just as the man's revolver went off. The shot went wild. Rob and the shooter grappled for the gun. Coop tried to take aim, but with Rob so close, he was afraid of hitting the other man.

Rob had jumped in to save him; surely he would've been shot and killed if Rob hadn't acted in that moment. So Coop looked around for a way to help. He spotted a broken branch. If he could grab it and hit the other shooter over his head or shoulder, Coop and Rob could get him under control, could have the advantage.

Coop was reaching for the branch when the tussling

men stumbled. Rob's foot hooked on a rock, the momentum throwing both men off-balance. They were too near the edge.

Coop shouted as both men disappeared over the edge of the precipice.

* * *

Thank you for reading FREEDOM'S DISTANT FRONTIER. I hope you loved Matt and Lily's romance. You'll see them again in HEART'S PERILOUS JOURNEY...

Keeping secrets is nearly impossible on an Oregon-bound wagon train. But Alice Spencer has kept a whopper from her protective brothers for months: she once fancied herself in love with her wealthy boss's grandson. Her brothers don't know *she's* the reason Rob Braddock came on this westward journey. Only that he's part of the reason they had to leave their home and friends behind. Her brothers will never forgive Rob—and neither can she.

The company is still weeks away from the Willamette Valley when Rob injures himself saving the youngest Spencer brother's life. Alice has no choice but to pay back the life-debt. She strikes a deal to help the injured Rob finish his journey to Oregon, at which point, they'll go their separate ways. All she has to do is keep from falling in love with him. Again.

- second chance romance
- he never stopped loving her
- different stations
- maid/wealthy

ONE CLICK HEART'S PERILOUS JOURNEY NOW >

For my Family, especially my Lily. You shine so bright and your heart is so big. I'm so proud of the young woman you are becoming.

Acknowledgments

To my excellent editor, D'Ann. Thank you for everything.

As always, I'm grateful to my proofreaders Lillian, Mary-Ellen, Benecia, and Shelley. A million thanks!

Want to connect online? Here's where you can find me:

GET NEW RELEASE ALERTS

Follow me on Amazon
Follow me on Bookbub
Follow me on Goodreads

CONNECT ON THE WEB

www.lacywilliams.net
lacy@lacywilliams.net

SOCIAL MEDIA

Also by Lacy Williams

WAGON TRAIN MATCHES

A Trail So Lonesome

Trail of Secrets

A Trail Untamed

Wild Heart's Haven

A Rugged Beauty

Love's Healing Path

Freedom's Distant Frontier

Heart's Perilous Journey

WIND RIVER HEARTS SERIES
(HISTORICAL ROMANCE)

Marrying Miss Marshal

Counterfeit Cowboy

Cowboy Pride

The Homesteader's Sweetheart

Courted by a Cowboy

Roping the Wrangler

Return of the Cowboy Doctor

The Wrangler's Inconvenient Wife

A Cowboy for Christmas

Her Convenient Cowboy

Her Cowboy Deputy

Catching the Cowgirl

The Cowboy's Honor

Winning the Schoolmarm

The Wrangler's Ready-Made Family

Christmas Homecoming

Heart of Gold

SUTTER'S HOLLOW SERIES
(CONTEMPORARY ROMANCE)

His Small-Town Girl

Secondhand Cowboy

The Cowgirl Next Door

COWBOY FAIRYTALES SERIES
(CONTEMPORARY FAIRYTALE ROMANCE)

Once Upon a Cowboy

Cowboy Charming

The Toad Prince

The Beastly Princess

The Lost Princess

Kissing Kelsey

Courting Carrie

Stealing Sarah

Keeping Kayla

Melting Megan

The Other Princess

The Prince's Matchmaker

HOMETOWN SWEETHEARTS SERIES (CONTEMPORARY ROMANCE)

Kissed by a Cowboy

Love Letters from Cowboy

Mistletoe Cowboy

The Bull Rider

The Brother

The Prodigal

Cowgirl for Keeps

Jingle Bell Cowgirl

Heart of a Cowgirl

3 Days with a Cowboy

Prodigal Cowgirl

Soldier Under the Mistletoe

The Nanny's Christmas Wish

The Rancher's Unexpected Gift

Someone Old

Someone New

Someone Borrowed

Someone Blue (newsletter subscribers only)

Ten Dates

Next Door Santa

Always a Bridesmaid

Love Lessons

NOT IN A SERIES

Wagon Train Sweetheart (historical romance)